The Line

The Line

A Novel

Courtney Brandt

iUniverse, Inc.
New York Lincoln Shanghai

The Line

iUniverse books may be ordered through booksellers or by contacting:

iUniverse
2021 Pine Lake Road, Suite 100
Lincoln, NE 68512
www.iuniverse.com
1-800-Authors (1-800-288-4677)

This is a work of fiction. All of the characters, names, incidents, organizations, and dialogue in this novel are either the products of the author's imagination or are used fictitiously.

ISBN-13: 978-0-595-42281-4 (pbk)
ISBN-13: 978-0-595-86618-2 (ebk)
ISBN-10: 0-595-42281-0 (pbk)
ISBN-10: 0-595-86618-2 (ebk)

Printed in the United States of America

Dedicated to …
The Brookwood HS Drum Line,
Past, present, and future.

Contents

Acknowledgements

Books don't get written by themselves. I mean, ok, yeah, it usually is just one author actually sitting and typing, but sometimes it's more than that. The Line is that novel ... which is why the Acknowledgements are in the front of this book.

Before I get any further, I have to thank all, each and every one of my readers at fanfiction.net. Literally, this story started out as an essay—a one shot idea that I posted to see if there was any interest. Many words, lots of reviews and a few crazy plot twists later, I finished The Line. During the process, certain individuals really separated themselves in their enthusiasm and optimism for both me and my writing.

Somewei, my ultimate enthusiast! I told you once that I lived for your reviews—it's still true. I hope you know how jealous I am of your mad talents ... your continued support of me is awesome.

Brokos, clarinet dude! I enjoy our daily talks, your sense of humor, your faith in my writing and I don't think I ever told you how completely flattered I am by the fact that you were partially inspired to write after reading my stuff. It's the biggest honor you could give an author!

Amy, where do I even begin? Sometimes, I'm not even sure if any of my books would get finished if it wasn't for you and your voice of sanity and reassurance. Every time we "talk," you prove to me that one of the reasons I started writing was so that we would "meet." You are a very talented individual with so much optimism—thanks for sharing it with me some of the time! And as a final thought—it only seems fair I use your definition for the Guard.

Out of cyberspace there are a few others I have to thank:

James and Gina, you each took the time out of your (very) busy lives to really read my book ... I hope you know how much that means to me.

Rachel Kuo, you might possibly be the single person I owe the most to! Thank you for, above all, listening and talking about my characters like they were real people. I owe you a lot more than a lunch at Chick-Fil-a.

Lisa, the original Drum Line girl ... we were a great team.

Mom and Dad, for support in all my endeavors.

Erin, for supporting me in your own way—now go read this book!

Shawna, for always asking about my writing.

Adam, for your wonderful and professional help with the cover.

And finally to Eric, thanks for the last minute definition idea! You support me every day by letting me be me.

Finally, to all those who are currently in marching band or are former band geeks like myself, I write for you!

PROLOGUE: TEN MINUTES

Marching band *n. A group of instrumental musicians who generally perform out-doors, who incorporate movement—usually some type of marching—with their musical performance. Instrumentation typically includes brass, woodwinds, and percussion instruments and the music usually incorporates a strong rhythmic component suitable for marching. If you value your life, do not utter the words "this one time at band camp" around a marching band member.*

Sophomore Lucy Karate took a deep breath and concentrated her moss green eyes on the black squiggles in front of her. The sheet music on the page was exactly the same it had been for the past ten months. The difference wasn't the music; it was the day. This was the day before auditions—her last opportunity to practice before her fate for the next school year was ultimately decided.

Recently turned sixteen Lucy Karate had been a member of the 250 strong Forrest Hills Flyers Marching Band for the past two seasons. Not as a clarinet player, or a trombonist, or one of the prissy Dance Line girls; Lucy had been a member of the Front Ensemble, the "Pit" in the Drum Line. She liked learning all the different mallet instruments the section had to offer, but was more than ready to join The Battery: Capital T, Capital B. The Battery was made up of instruments who actually marched on the field. Earning a spot on The Battery had been just a dream for the past year. Back in middle school when she joined the band, Lucy had chosen to play the oboe. It was just her luck that she has picked the *one* instrument that was incapable of marching. Most oboists learned to play the flute or piccolo, but not Lucy. There was some call; some deep pull of the Drum Line that had made her chose the section. Given that she could already read music and mallets weren't the most difficult instruments to learn, the band directors had let the forceful brunette into the predominantly male section, hoping she would have a calming influence. Entering high school, Lucy would have never guessed that she would become borderline obsessive with all things percussion. During auditions for the previous season, she had been devastated to be placed on the Front Line for another year.

Cymbals … maybe, or possibly bass … Lucy thought to herself when she started picturing her junior year. She wasn't going to kid herself about tenors or snare.

The Forrest Hills High School Drum Line was an unbelievably talented group. They had a number of percussionists make All State Band every year. Lucy knew she would be happy just to get on the field. She wanted her junior year to be worth something. Lots of great things were going to happen during the 11th grade—making use of her month old drivers license, becoming an upperclassman, hopefully going to Prom, getting her first job, her first AP classes, starting to worry about which college she was going to attend …

Concentrate Lucy. All that can wait. This is about the Line now.

Down Under. The petite sophomore knew this particular selection was the one that would make or break her audition. Unlike the rest of the guys on the Line, Lucy preferred to practice by herself. Ever since the previous season had ended, Lucy had taken her practice pad and sticks into the garage and practiced an hour or more every day. She downloaded reams of music from the Internet, listened to cadences, and watched DCI shows almost weekly. She had never been more committed to anything in her entire life. Lucy finally put the music away.

I am SO not getting any sleep tonight.

Like a metronome at 140 beats per minute, the next day passed quickly. Lucy didn't even bother trying to concentrate in her classes. She kept going over the audition pieces in her head, trying to visualize herself playing them perfectly. After school, the potential drummers gathered outside the band room. With only five seniors graduating there wasn't a lot of room for movement on the Line. The Battery, while larger than many high school percussion sections, was only made up of six snares, four tenors, five basses, and seven cymbals with another eight or so in the Pit. Lucy nervously went around the corner and began warming up on her practice pad. Far too soon, she heard her name called.

Lucy walked into the spacious band room with her hands behind her back. She was trying to calm herself, willing her hands to stop shaking. In front of her stood a practice table, and in front of that, The Judges. The Drum Line judiciary committee included: the two band directors, Mr. Izzo and Mr. Beard, Henry the percussion instructor, and one of the local percussion teachers, Mr. DiBonaventura. Lucy looked at the table, noting that it was far too tall for her 5 feet 4 inches. Henry grinned and stood up on Lucy's behalf, moving the director's podium for Lucy to stand on. Taking a step up, it was more than enough, and Lucy now towered over the judges.

Henry said politely, "If you would please play the two prepared pieces. You will then be asked to sight read a short selection."

Since I've probably already blown this, then I guess I have nothing to lose.

Hey now. You did not waste *weeks* of your life practicing to have an attitude like that!

And you would be?

Just consider me your inner percussionist. So, make me proud girl—go out there and kick some ass!

Fine. Let's show 'em what this oboist can do.

As if in a trance, Lucy played the two prepared pieces. After six months of practicing every day, the rhythms poured out of her hands. Lucy stopped. The judges noted her scores.

Henry continued, "Please turn over the piece in front of you. You will have ninety seconds to review the music."

The ninety seconds passed in a blur. If there was one thing Lucy needed practice at, it was sight-reading. She had dreaded this part of the audition.

"You may begin."

She persevered through the piece as best she could, then it was over and Mr. Izzo was saying, "Thanks for coming in, Lucy. Positions will be posted tomorrow after school."

Lucy stammered, "Thanks."

She stumbled out of the room. The whole thing had taken less than ten minutes. It didn't matter that she had spent weeks of her life practicing in the past year. All that mattered were the past ten minutes. However, reflecting on what had happened, Lucy was not discouraged. She had solidly played both of the audition pieces. She tried to convince herself that the sight-reading didn't really matter and that it was mainly for the placement of the quints and snares.

Lucy gathered her messenger bag and went outside to wait in front of the school. Listening to her iPod, she was trying her best to concentrate on her history homework. She had the sound up so loud that she jumped when someone tapped her on the shoulder. Lucy looked next to her and saw the redheaded heartthrob of the entire marching band, cymbal player Nevada Petersen, looking over her shoulder. She took off her headphones, willing herself not to blush.

"How'd you do, Luce?" Nevada asked.

"Good, I think. You?" *He knows my name?* As a member of the Pit, Lucy didn't get to interact with The Battery much last season and was surprised the cute upcoming senior even remembered her name.

"Not sure. As much as I want quints, I think they're going to stick me in charge of the cymbals."

"Would that be so bad?" Lucy gave him a hopeful smile.

"I guess not."

Glimpsing a familiar car approaching, Lucy wanted to curse under breath as her Mom pulled up.

Thanks Mom, I've been waiting forever to talk to Nevada, and here he is talking to me and you decide to show up!

Sighing, Lucy collected her homework and headed to the car, "Well …"

"I hope you make The Battery, Lucy. We're definitely going to need something of a female influence next season," Nevada said with a wink.

Lucy was completely embarrassed when her cheeks flushed, "Thanks. See you at Warm-up Week."

"Yup."

Lucy got in the car, smiling and hoping that her conversation with Nevada was some sort of good omen for the results tomorrow.

"Who was that?" asked Lucy's mom, Becky.

"Umm … he's on the Line."

"Is he graduating in May or will you be seeing him next season?"

"He'll be a senior."

"He's cute."

"Mo-oom." It was amazing how perceptive her mother could be sometimes. Since her freshman year, Lucy had been carrying an Olympic sized torch for the attractive drummer. She had watched, from a distance, as Nevada had dated a string of girls in the marching band, mostly from the pretty Auxiliary sections.

"Ok, ok, how did auditions go?"

"Good enough. I guess we'll find out tomorrow."

The following day, Lucy tapped her pencil in Economics class impatiently. She glanced at her chipped pink nail polish and ragged fingernails.

How am I going to make it through the whole day just sitting and wondering about a stupid piece of paper?

Uh … easy? Go down there and see if it's been posted.

You mean just leave class?

Now you're catching on!

She raised her hand timidly, "Can I go to the bathroom?"

Dr. Knott nodded; he was too busy trying to make the laws of supply and demand interesting to a bunch of sophomores.

Lucy walked through the deserted halls and found herself in front of the band room. She approached the band director's office—where lists of this importance were usually posted and sighed—no list yet.

Mr. Izzo was on the phone in his office. He saw Lucy outside and, hardly believing what he was doing, Lucy watched as he held up two fingers. Then he mouthed the word, "Bass."

Lucy choked back an excited scream and a grin lit up her entire face.

DRUM LINE

(First practice—next Monday after school!
*denotes section Lieutenant)

SNARES

*Jerm (Captain)

Billy

Adam

James

Herschel

Gardner

QUINTS

*Doug

Tom

Ewan

Andy

BASS

Mark (1st)

Lucy (2nd)

*Lance (3rd)

Nathan (4th)

Jared (5th)

CYMBALS

*Nevada

Morty

Kevin

Scott

Thomas

Ben

Donovan

PIT

*Molly

Hank

Vince

Sean

Doyle

Chad

Christopher

After school that day, the percussionists crowded around the list. There was some obvious surprise at Lucy's assigned slot. The newly christened second bass drummer tried to ignore some of the ruder comments, recognizing that this was a weird time of year on the Line. Although everyone was friendly during the season, around auditions, friendships were put on a temporary hiatus. Lucy was also not surprised to see she was the only girl on The Battery. She walked away from the list, taking a mental snapshot. All those hours of practicing paid off on a simple piece of paper.

1

THE SEASON BEGINS

Drum Line, Drumline, The Line n. *A group of percussionists who play a variety of percussion instruments in a marching band usually made up of both a Front Line and Battery. This group sets the beat and rhythms for the rest of the larger marching unit and most often recognized by their cocky smiles and confident attitudes. A "line" may also refer to one particular section within the drum line i.e. the tenor, snare or bass line.*

On a sweltering afternoon in August, Lucy lugged her thirty-pound bass drum to her car, the "Matt Damon," a blue Chevrolet Cavalier that was in desperate need of a paint job. She had taken the big drum home over the summer to try and get used to the weight. Wanting to make sure the guys didn't forget her gender, Lucy had secured a flashy Tinkerbell sticker to her carrier. She looked at the metal contraption—it was a tradition to put your initials on it to mark your season. Lucy smiled, remembering the seniors who had made her freshman and sophomore years such fun.

Although Lucy had thought it would take forever for her junior year to start, the summer had flown by in a blur. Lucy and one of her best friends, Mandy, a legs for miles blond on Color Guard, had both gotten jobs at the local pizza place. They had flirted their way through the minimum wage hours with the delivery boys. When she wasn't working, Lucy kept in touch with friends via IM and the occasional party.

Lucy had been waiting for this day for so long, she could hardly believe that it was finally the first practice of the season. The brunette drove up to the high school and took a deep breath, mentally preparing herself for the next couple of hours. In the middle of her calming thoughts, a large blue minivan with racing stripes pulled up next to her. Only one person at this school drove that car, Tom Finnegan, a junior and one of her best friends. They shared a smile across their cars. Ever since the band trip to Disneyland their freshman year, Tom and Lucy had been close to inseparable. They both had a bizarre sense of humor that no one else really seemed to get. Tom, forever failing the gifted classes that he signed up for, relied on Lucy's ability to study and get him to concentrate in order not to flunk whatever grade they were in. Lucy noted that Tom was quite tan after working the entire summer as a lifeguard. She rolled her eyes thinking of his goofy cuteness that had probably earned him quite a female following at the local pool. He opened his trunk and pulled out his quints. They both pulled down their black Oakley sunglasses (THE eye wear of choice for Battery members) and together they walked towards the band room.

Tom asked, "You ready for this?"

Lucy replied with a good smattering of sarcasm, "Are you kidding? I was born ready."

The crowded band room was full of people. Lieutenants and Captains tried, with varying degrees of success, to corral their sections together. Finally, Fred, one of the Drum Majors, fellow junior, and Lucy's friend since fifth grade, clapped his hands for attention. He gave a stirring speech about how great the season was going to be and how every person in the band made a difference. The band then broke into sectionals and the Line marched out in front of the school to their traditional warm up spot where Henry was waiting for them. Lucy walked with Molly and caught up with the only other source of estrogen on the Line.

"What do you think he's going to say?" Lucy asked, suddenly nervous.

"Nothing," Molly replied honestly.

As Forrest Hills' Instructor for three years, Henry didn't need to give a speech this early in the season. They all knew he expected the best and wouldn't accept anything less. He wrote all their music, tuned them, and made sure they were one of the best high school Drum Lines in the nation. The Battery warmed up together while the Pit went inside to work on their mallet technique. They went over the basic rudiments and drills that everyone had learned during Warm-up Week. Knowing Eight on a Hand by heart and protected by the dark tint of her sunglasses, Lucy considered her fellow basses.

Mark stood in front of her on first bass. A cocky, cute sophomore, Mark was arrogant as hell and had a mouth like a sailor. Fortunately, Mark had long ago classified her as "cute," which meant their relationship thus far was made up almost entirely of sexual innuendoes and third grade flirting techniques like stealing each other's mallets.

That reminds me …

Lucy snuck a look at Henry, who was busy talking to the quints. She leaned forward and flicked Mark's ear.

Behind Lucy on third bass was her Lieutenant, Lance. Lance had been on the bass line last year and was the only one returning to the section. He was also a sophomore. Tall, with dark hair, and like most percussionists she knew, overly confident (when it came to drumming at least) he lead their sectionals and tried to keep Lucy and Mark from killing each other.

Behind Lance on fourth bass was dark haired nerdy cute Nathan.

I can't believe I used to be obsessed with him …

Not one of your finest moments.

It didn't end that badly.

Well, it wasn't for lack of you trying, was it?

…

Bringing up the end of the basses was Jared. Lovable Jared. Pacifist Jared. Jared liked two things in life: drumming and the band Less Than Jake. He played the big fifth bass. Altogether, the basses were by far the most eclectic section in the Line.

Lucy couldn't help it as her eyes were drawn to the cymbal line. She hadn't seen Nevada all summer and was simply staring at him behind her dark sunglasses.

If anything, he looks better than I remember.

Even with buckets of sweat pouring off his muscular arms?

Especially then.

Henry held up a stick signaling the last run through of the warm up. Lucy guiltily snapped back to attention as she clicked her mallets against her drum. In this week before Band Camp, the Line was mainly getting together to review cadences and get their chops back before they received their music for this year's halftime show. Basically, for a short time, there wasn't a lot to do. It was a time, so early in the season, that there was no history established with the Line. No one had started to get on each other's nerves, there were no fights over girls, and there was no blaming over dropped sticks or notes. It was a golden time in the season that wouldn't last long. Henry looked at all of them, "Great first practice, guys. I have big plans for this season. I'll see you all at band camp."

Before she realized it, Lucy's first official band practice was over. She was sweaty and a little sore, but overall, very satisfied with the way things had went. So far, she had kept up her part as one-fifth of the bass line. She joked around with the guys as they put their equipment away in the large room just off the band room that was the percussion headquarters. Not only a place to store their instruments, it was *the* location for inside jokes, blowing off steam, and occasionally, a place to sleep between classes.

Lucy met up with Mandy and Gina, the third of the Three Musketeers, and also a talented majorette in her own right. In the off-season (and the origination of their friendship), Gina was first chair bassoon and Mandy was co-first chair clarinet in the Honor Band, joining Lucy and her oboe in the first row. The three chatted about where they were going to go after practice. Lucy knew that the unofficial hang out for the upperclassmen on The Battery (and its endless stream of groupies) was the local Waffle House. She had been there once the year before, when the Line had gone out en masse after winning an important competition.

Lucy looked at her friends, "Let's say we start the year out differently. Let's go to WaHo."

Lucy knew that she wouldn't hear a lot of arguments. Mandy had confessed earlier that summer to a growing crush on Jerm (the Drum Line Captain, who only responded to Jeremiah when the band directors called him that) and Gina was happy to go along wherever the fun was. They all piled into Gina's red Hybrid Civic and took off.

During the ride over they gossiped about what had gone on over the summer and, more importantly, the new trumpet player that had shown up to practice today. No one knew his name yet, but they would ask their spies in the section all about him. A cute, talented horn player would most certainly be the source of competition between the girls of the Auxiliaries (Color Guard, Dance Line, and Majorettes) and the band girls. By the time they reached Waffle House, Gina had made her mind up to get to know him better.

Most of the Line had arrived before the girls did. Unfortunately, that meant a lot of the Auxiliaries had also shown up already. The girls were shameless in their attempt to get attention from the drummers. For the most part, the girls in the "pretty sections" were the sworn enemies of Lucy and Molly. These girls didn't realize they had to really gain *their* respect first, before going after one the guys on the Line. Lucy knew she was a walking contradiction, considering her best friends in the world were Auxiliary members themselves, but she chose to think of them as musicians first and Guard and Majorettes second.

Jerm, seated in the middle of the large corner booth, was already talking about the year ahead, "The way I figure it, South is the only Line we really have to worry about. You saw them all last year."

The Drum Line Captain was speaking about the cross-town rival Line—South Washington High School. He wasn't speaking of any band competition or football game; he was looking forward to November when the Indoor drum line battles would start. Their Lines were in a constant struggle for first place. From Lucy's first day in the Line, it had been drilled into her that they had to beat South and that all drummers from South were not to be trusted.

The guys all nodded in agreement. Jerm's fellow seniors definitely wanted to go out on a high note. At that moment, Lucy, Gina, and Mandy walked through the door. Lucy stopped and scanned the room. She had been on the Line for two years and had developed some close friendships with some of the other juniors. However, she had never hung out socially with the seniors. From a purely percussion standpoint, they were intimidating. Lucy wanted to approach them, but didn't want to risk being shot down in front of her friends. Across the crowded diner, the Auxiliary girls shot death stares at Lucy, Gina, and Mandy.

Just like at the lunch table during their Fifth period percussion class, there was a fair amount of politics that existed in the seating of this particular Waffle House. It wasn't so bad that it broke down into sections, but the seniors definitely had their own table. After the senior table, the tables were classified by "cool" juniors, "cool" sophomores, "not-so-cool" juniors and sophomores and finally, freshman. As the only girl on The Battery, Lucy knew she was pushing her luck with any of the tables, even though she had been friends with some of these guys since seventh grade.

Stupid guys and their stupid testosterone. Stupid hierarchy.

Lucy pulled Gina and Mandy toward the freshman table. There was no way fourteen-year-old boys were going to turn down a female, even if she was the only girl on The Battery.

"What's up, dudes?" Lucy casually sat down and started talking to the younger boys about their upcoming first year in high school.

"Can you believe her?" asked Adam from across the room. The guys watched as Lucy flirted with the younger Pit and cymbal members.

Jerm looked up, momentarily entranced by the beautiful Mandy, before replying, "I don't think it's so bad, guys. She was fine at practice today. In fact, the bass line is sounding better than it has in years."

Nevada spoke up, smiling, "Let's invite her over. You know, for the sake of Battery peace and all that."

Five pairs of eyes looked over at Jerm. He was their leader both on and off the field. Jerm considered Lucy for a minute. He hadn't really taken much notice until her appearance on the Battery this year. Girls on the Line could be trouble. There was something about entirely too many guy hormones and not enough girl hormones to offset all the testosterone. Rarely was there a fight over a drum line girl, but Lucy was cute, and it could mean that some tempers would flare. On the other hand, Lucy's friend Mandy was HOT. This could be his only way to meet her. Jerm called out, "Lucy!"

Lucy, engrossed in making the younger boys laugh and eating away at her scattered-smothered-covered hash browns, almost didn't realize someone was calling her name. Recognizing her Captain's voice, she tried to play it as cool as possible replied, "Yes, Jerm?"

"Why don't you come sit over here?" Jerm asked.

Never one to leave her girlfriends behind, Lucy said, "Do you have room for my friends?"

Scruffy Doug yelled, "Come on—we don't have all night!"

The girls casually said their good byes to the freshman table, smiled smugly at the other girls in the diner, who were hoping to get spots at the table themselves, and squeezed into the crowded booth. Lucy and the girls chatted away with the seniors until curfew. There was never a lull in conversation. As with most people in marching band, the guys and girls actually had a lot of overlapping friends. Plus, the seniors were able to fill in the juniors about some of the teachers they would have in the following year. Lucy also found herself curiously more attracted than usual to Nevada. She had locked eyes with him a few times during the night and did her best to hold his hazel gaze. She had always considered him out of her league, but there was something different about tonight. Somehow, the cymbal player seemed attainable.

And why shouldn't he be?

Well, it's just that he's Nevada …

And you're not good enough?

No.

Then what?

Hey, would you look at the time? It's almost curfew.

Fine, but this isn't over.

Saying their goodbyes, Gina and Lucy walked outside and hopped in the Civic. As they waited for the third door to slam, the girls realized Mandy was still deep in conversation with Jerm. Mandy skipped up to the car and said cheerfully, "Jerm is going to give me a ride home! He lives in my direction anyway."

Gina and Lucy shared a look and rolled their eyes, knowing very well that Jerm and Mandy didn't live *that* close to each other. Gina dropped Lucy at her car in the school parking lot. Lucy pulled up her favorite "Sing Along" playlist on her iPod and drove home, pondering this seemingly good start to her junior year. She had made The Battery. She had gotten her first real job. Now, as Lucy sang along with Urge Overkill's "You'll Be A Woman Soon," it was time to start worrying about Homecoming. Lucy sighed; she hadn't ever had a good time at this dance. It just seemed that the end of October was always an awkward time of year for her when it came to guys.

Let's be honest Luce, it's always an awkward time of year when it comes to guys with you ...

There's always Nevada. Can you imagine how good he would look dressed up?

*No, guys on the Line are for **flirting only**.*

After a failed attempt at a relationship with Nathan and a brief flirtation with Tom, Lucy had made a pact with herself not to get involved with members of her section. She knew it was best to just be the token girl and not anyone's official girlfriend. Something strange always accompanied the label. While changing for an Indoor competition last year in the ladies room (as usual, it was entirely empty), she and Molly had decided that their role on the Line was part psychiatrist, part matchmaker, and full time masseuse. The girls were there on the long rides back from a competition to massage those sore shoulders and arms. The favor was almost universally returned and when it came November and December and the bus rides were chilly, who better to snuggle down with than a cute drummer? As long as you remembered it didn't mean anything, no one got hurt.

Lucy arrived at her house, but didn't feel like going to sleep right away. Her thoughts kept straying towards potential guys she wanted to date this year. Lucy was a big fan of the crush. She could hardly wait for school to begin again and she could begin seeing her crushes on a regular basis. Other than Nevada, she had a long running crush on none other than the class president, Murray. The super smart cutie was not in band, only in her classes, and had caught her attention in gifted Biology their freshman year. She wondered what Murray had been up to this summer. As the cute head of the class and all around nice guy, she knew many people that held a torch for him. Sighing, Lucy had long ago realized that crushes were not always about returned love. Sometimes it was just fun to know that there was a guy out there who could make your entire day by a smile or conversation.

Sometimes, that's all you have going for you ...

2

BAND CAMP

bass drum *n. A large drum having a cylindrical body and two heads and producing a low, resonant sound. The pitched bass drum is generally used in marching bands and drum corps. This particular type of drum is tuned to a specific pitch and is typically played in a set of three to six drums. The second bass drummer has a particularly important position for setting the downbeat, tempo, and diagonal of the drill.*

A few days later, Lucy waved goodbye to her parents and younger brother, Craig, as Tom pulled away from her house. She wasn't quite sure how she had managed to convince her parents to let her crazy friend drive her up to Band Camp, but she was happy they had agreed. The Forrest Hills High School band camp was held two hours away at a small college. The large band completely took over the college for the week—using every inch of the campus—the dorm rooms for sleeping, the dining hall, classrooms for practice, and gardens for taking "hot walks." Lucy looked over at Tom and smiled, looking forward to this mini-road trip. Plus, one of the true signs of being an upperclassman was NOT having your parents drive you up to band camp.

Tom winked and said, "We have to make a quick stop."

Lucy knew what that meant. Tom would not drive anywhere further than five miles without beef jerky and a Big Gulp from the local Quick Trip. But before Lucy could do or say much of anything, Tom had quickly added Nevada, Ewan, and Nathan to the car.

At least I'll be pulling up in style …

Lucy smiled to herself as she pictured the look of jealousy on many a girl's face who would like a spot in the minivan.

The road trip was filled with establishing new inside jokes, reciting lines from favorite movies, mooning other cars, listening to Tom's band Eight Cadet (a ska-influenced group whose "gigs" had so far included a neighborhood block party and a bar mitzvah) newest recording, talking about the season ahead and, a sigh-worthy, all too brief nap on Nevada's broad shoulder. In the early afternoon, the party wagon pulled up to the girls' dorm. Lucy waved goodbye to the guys as she went to check in. The bass drummer swept into the lobby as the girls outside watched her section mates pull away. Lucy was rooming in a triple with Mandy and Gina, who were arriving together after making a planned stop at the nearby outlet mall. After Lucy put her things away, she stretched out on the bed, closing her eyes and remembering previous band camps: getting dunked in large bins of ice, crushing on hot upperclassmen, learning music and trying to memorize it as fast as possible, laughing hysterically at the planned night activities, flirting with underclassmen, meeting people from different schools, making new friends and trying her best to go on as few hours sleep as possible.

Post band camp

Dear Diary,

First of all, please pardon the extreme stream of consciousness style of this entry. I haven't got a lot of sleep this week! But, as usual, it was totally and completely worth it.

So, first of all, learning the show was a different experience than I thought it was going to be. Sure, it was hot and sweaty, but it's was also pretty amazing when you think of it—250 people on a field, actually going where they are supposed to go all while playing memorized music! (BTW, the show's theme this year is 'A Night At the Movies' including: Mission Impossible, Pink Panther, and James Bond—the drum solo takes place in the 2nd song—we've learned the music, but haven't learned the drill yet). Learning the music and the formations was a process that took awhile, but that I'm proud to say we all accomplished it and I can't wait to see how far we're going to go! So, of course, like any good band camp, there was more than just marching.

First of all, can I just say how much I hate Mark? We fight so much that the rest of the basses have dubbed us Mr. and Mrs. DeMatteo. (Yes, I, of course, have taken his last name.) There is not ONE thing we can agree on. The tempo (which I set), dressing the line (I decide how sharp the diagonal will be), how hot it is, how cold it is, visuals … That being said, we can have moments when it's Lucy and Mark vs. the World … where we have a never-ending stream of inside jokes, non-stop flirting and the rest of the basses have no idea what is going on between 1st and 2nd. Realistically, I'd say it's about 30/70 for the whole love/hate thing. However, Mark does help me realize I'm a lot tougher than I used to be. Lucy from two years ago probably would have run off crying, but Junior Lucy has a quick bitchy response ready. I think Lance is getting close to killing us …

Mandy and I tried to keep each other on track (and mostly failing) to study for our upcoming AP U.S. History class. Hey—not our fault! We had every intention of studying every day, but as soon as we took those books out someone was there to distract us. She confided in me that things are going well between she and Jerm …

Gina was also up to some awesomeness. I'm so proud of this girl. She earned the coveted spot of feature twirler this year. I watch her and I'm amazed by the crazy amount of things she can do with a baton. Seriously, she can get some height on that thing. She also received some male attention this week. I noticed her and Jonathan (the cute trumpet player has a name!) together a few times.

Finally, sigh, Nevada. Beautiful, redheaded, Christian Bale-esque Nevada. Remember how I said that I wouldn't date (ok, I could like them I just couldn't do anything about it) anyone on the Line? Well, I'm thinking maybe I should amend that. It all started on the trip up and then he was just always there at the end of practice ready to give me a back massage (definitely necessary after a long day and a heavy drum), sitting next to me at the night activities, piggy back rides anywhere I wanted … I know, this could all just be flirting, but is it wrong if I want it to be more? I hope I'm not reading into things. I have a big tendency to do that. But still, I REALLY, REALLY want something to happen. And it almost did once or twice or maybe it didn't! I can't tell!!!! For someone who is around guys all the time, I certainly wonder why I can't read the ones I'm interested in. Molly thinks that for sure he does like me, but what if he doesn't and I end up making a big fool of myself?

Which brings me to my big school-is-almost-starting resolution. I'm not sure if it's my being on The Battery, the change of scenery from the field, or that new inner percussionist constantly in my ear, but I am ready for a change this year. Reading what I JUST finished writing, I feel like a whiny little underclassmen. I want to take some risks in the romance department this year, because let's face it, where has having a crush gotten me so far? I want to be a normal high school girl and go on dates and have a boyfriend. I don't want to be some lame chick who just waits for things and then never gets anywhere, because really, is that who I still am? I don't want to be always known as Lucy Karate, The Good Friend. Lucy, never with a boyfriend. Lucy, awww, wouldn't she be cute with so and so? After this week, I think I've proven to myself that I'm braver and stronger and deserve more. If I have to go out and make some things happen, then so be it. So there, it's official. I, Lucy Karate, will take a risk this year when it comes to the opposite sex, <u>no matter what.</u>

Ta for now,
Lucy

Lucy put her diary away, determined to keep the promise she had made to herself and firm in her decision not to be the Lucy she had been for the past two years, but Lucy Karate, kick ass girl on The Battery with plenty of choices when it came boys.

What are you waiting for?

Just hours ago, she had been at band camp. Now here she sat, the summer slowly slipping away and risks were waiting to be taken. Lucy had to get out of the house. With the exception of people named after states, there was no one in particular she wanted to see. Ponytail swishing, she went down to check the paper to see if any good movies were playing. Glancing at the clock, there was still time to make the matinee at her favorite dollar theater. She grabbed her keys, shouting out, "Hey Mom, I'm going to see a movie!"

"You still have energy after band camp?" her Mom's voice called out after her.

"Believe it or not, I do. I'll be home in time for dinner!"

Lucy pulled up to the theater. The dollar theater used to be a grand movie palace in the 1950's and still held some of the old Hollywood glamour. She bought a ticket, then went to the counter and purchased her traditional movie treats—Swedish fish and a Diet Coke, and went in to find a seat. The theater was not very full. She took a seat near the front. Before the movie started, Lucy began randomly tapping out a cadence on her knee. It was such a subconscious thing for her after the past week; and she was so into the notes she didn't realize someone else was tapping along with her. Lucy stopped and turned around. Behind her was a *very* cute boy. He was tall, as Lucy quickly noticed, with cropped dark hair and twinkling cobalt blue eyes. He looked familiar ... he didn't go to Forrest Hills, but she knew she recognized him from somewhere. Lucy blushed, "Sorry."

What do you mean sorry? What could you possibly be sorry about? It's a free country and you're allowed to—

Lucy's inner struggle was interrupted when the Cute Boy said, "I don't mind. Do you drum?"

Lucy froze. While she was crazy proud of being a drummer, there was the risk that the Cute Boy would think she was some sort of unfeminine freak if she told him the truth.

Listen, I don't care what you say, as long as you continue talking to him.

She decided to play it safe, "No, I was just tapping."

"Sounded like a cadence to me. In fact, that sounded quite a lot like the Cavaliers ..."

"No, what's a cadence?" Lucy cut him off innocently, knowing perfectly well she *had* been tapping out Cavvies."

"It's a ... never mind." The cute guy was quiet.

Frick! What's a girl to do?

What would Mandy and Gina do?

If I were Gina or Mandy, I would probably already have him sitting next to me buying me a gynormous popcorn.

Lucy heard herself blurting out, "Swedish fish!"

"What?" asked the cute boy, eyes twinkling again.

"Would you like a Swedish fish? They're really good," Lucy said lamely.

I'm sure if that technically counts as a risk, but at least you are attempting something ...

"Sure. Mind if I sit next to you? I mean, you're not saving that seat for your boyfriend or something are you?" Cute Boy asked, hinting he was definitely hoping there was NOT someone coming to sit next to Lucy.

"No, just me and the fish. You're more than welcome to join us."

The Cute Boy moved down a row and sat right next to her.

"Sam," he said holding out his hand.

"Lucy," she said, shaking his hand, and not backing off any when she squeezed his hand.

Lucy desperately wanted to learn more about Sam, but the house lights went down and the movie started. Lucy was hyper aware of his presence next to hers.

You know, really taking a risk would be reaching over and holding his hand ...

Baby steps, ok? I *am* sitting next to him. Isn't that enough?

Well, you need to chat him up—there's something about him that's definitely familiar.

This close to Sam, Lucy knew there was no way she was going to concentrate on the film. She wracked her brain, trying to come up with where the cute boy sitting next to her was from ... and then the truth hit her like a bucket of cold water. Sam wasn't just any Sam. The young man sitting next to her was none other than the *Captain of South Washington's Drum Line!*

Ok, deep breaths, he obviously doesn't recognize you. You can still get out of here without anyone from your Line knowing what you did.

Any semblance of concentration Lucy currently had was broken when Sam reached over and began softly stroking the back of her hand. Goosebumps shot up her arm and treasonous thoughts snuck into her head.

So what if I date him?

Umm ... have you looked up Benedict Arnold in the dictionary? Maybe they're going to print your face instead of his.

How would anyone from my Line know, and furthermore, who cares if I want to date another drummer?

You're not *actually* considering seeing him again, are you?

That question was easily answered when Sam stretched his arm around Lucy's shoulders.

You were saying ...?

Leaning into Sam's strong arm, it seemed like Lucy blinked and the movie was over.

"How'd you like it?" Sam asked as they walked into the lobby.

"Umm, well I think it was a lot better than a lot of the stuff that's out there. I like the director a lot. I hope she does more things soon."

"Yeah, me too."

Lucy gulped at the very obvious Awkward Silence.

Sam finally spoke up, "So, can I walk you to your car?"

Lucy thought a second. Immediately she thought of the Pearl drum logo that was clearly visible on her bumper. She had put it there proudly when she had seen her name listed under the bass category in the band room earlier that year. Sam would no doubt recognize the logo and wonder how it got there if she wasn't a drummer.

What would be so wrong with telling him the truth?

If *I* was Captain of South's Line, I wouldn't be seen *near* anyone from Forrest Hills. I especially would not want to date someone from their Line.

*But why don't you make that **his** decision?*

Because I really want to see him again!

So, you're going to pretend to be someone you're not? That's not cool.

Well, so far being 'cool' has gotten me approximately zero boyfriends and a whole lot of lonely weekends.

Fine. So, what about the sticker?

Got it. It's my 'older brother's' hand-me-down car!

"I'd like that," Lucy finally responded, summoning all the courage she had and desperately trying to send subconscious signals to Sam that she wouldn't mind seeing him again.

They walked to the parking lot. Sam saw the logo, and questioned doubtfully, "You sure you're not a drummer?"

Lucy casually smiled, "The car used to be my brother's."

And by used to, I mean, 'will one day be' my brother's.

"Really? Was he ever on Drum Line?"

Lucy smoothly replied, "As a matter of fact he was. He was on quints two years at Forrest Hills."

"You go to Forrest Hills?" Sam's eyebrows went up and the tone in his voice changed.

"Yes, and I suppose you're going to tell me you go to South?" Lucy questioned in what she hoped was an honest tone.

"Yes, I do."

Again Awkward Silence.

Lucy sighed and even though she felt like kicking her tire in frustration, she said neutrally, "Well, I have to get home. My parents are expecting me for dinner."

She slowly opened her car door; waiting, hoping desperately that Sam would try to stop her. He didn't. *Damn school rivalries.* Lucy drove out of the parking lot and stopped at a red light, trying not focus on what just happened.

*You could've asked **him** out.*

I think I've come far enough away from my comfort bubble today, thank you very much. Do I need to remind you that I literally *just* made that resolution?

Hello? What did you have to lose back there? You'll never see him again!

Until October when our Lines face off against each other! Believe me, this way is safer for everyone involved.

Safer? Maybe. More fun? Definitely not.

Her thoughts were interrupted as she heard a car beeping next to her. It was Sam! He had his window rolled down and motioned for her to do the same thing. Lucy tried to look nonchalant as she hurried to get her window down.

Sam yelled, "What's your number?"

Lucy smiled; this was more like it, "555-0317."

Sam called out, "I'll call you soon—I owe you some Swedish fish!" and drove away.

Lucy drove home singing. Walking into the house, she saw a note in the kitchen from her Mom. Nevada had called. As if her heart hadn't been through enough today, this definitely got it pumping again.

3

ALLEGRO

Tenor drums n. A marching percussion instrument commonly seen as mounted sets of 3-6 drums, allowing one person to carry and play multiple drums simultaneously. Can also be referred to as tenors, quads, quints, or squints. These drums are played on both an x and y axis i.e. not only do you have to have proper up and down technique, side to side playing must also be correct.

Lucy took a deep breath. Nevada called. So what? It's not like she'd never talked to a guy on the phone before. She and Fred once talked for three hours on one very rainy Saturday and then there was the infamous "asleep" phone call she and Tom had shared their freshman year.

OK, I don't want to seem like I'm totally desperate, so I won't call back until tomorrow ... ok, later tonight, ok, as soon as dinner is over.

And?

And, what?

Aren't you going to ask him out or something?

Why?

Isn't that the risky thing to do?

Sheesh, one day at a time. Isn't trying to date the Captain of my rival Drum Line enough?

Lucy wondered what she awoken in her subconscious. Grabbing her earpiece after dinner, Lucy walked outside with the family dog, Pam, a fawn pug. She nervously dialed Nevada's number, then hung up, clearing the phone. Wiping sweaty palms on her khaki shorts, she punched the numbers in again ... and deleted the numbers again. She was about to redial for the seventh time when her phone started ringing. Lucy almost dropped the phone. Glancing at the screen, she saw a local area code, but didn't recognize the number.

"Hello?" she asked tentatively.

"Is this Lucy?"

Lucy heard a guy's husky voice on the other end, but she wasn't sure who it was, "Yes."

"Hey Lucy—it's Sam, from earlier today."

"Oh hey." Lucy wanted to play it cool, even though her heart was (again) erratically pounding in her chest. She briefly wondered if she was too young to be at risk for a heart attack.

"Listen, I feel kind of crappy about how I was earlier today. I mean, just because you go to Forrest Hills, it doesn't necessarily mean that you're automatically evil or anything."

"And just because you go to South doesn't mean you're automatically a loser or anything," Lucy said smiling.

"Touché. Well, anyway, I was wondering if you wanted to maybe get some ice cream next Monday? Kind of a 'we got through the first day of school thing.'"

"Scoop It Up?"

"How did you know?"

"Hey, even though I go to Forrest Hills, I may know something about the best ice cream in town."

"No arguments here. However, I'm not sure if they have Swedish fish as a topping."

"That's okay."

"So, pick you up sevenish?"

"Sounds good. Call me after school on Monday to get my address." Lucy's head was spinning. She doubted seriously she could wait that long to talk to him, but didn't want to seem too desperate to talk, so she tried to casually ask, "Are you ever online at all?"

"Sometimes. What's your screen name?"

Crap. "It's um, bassgirl17."

"Do you play the guitar?"

"I'm, um, just starting to learn."

"Awesome. Did you know I was in a band? Besides marching, I mean."

"No. Are you the drummer extraordinaire?"

Sam laughed, "Something like that. We just got together. So, no gigs yet. All we've done is come up with the name."

"Which is?"

"Runaway Truck Ramp."

"That's awesome." Lucy's phone beeped in her ear. She looked at the screen—it was Mandy, "Well, hey, I actually have to take this other call. Talk to you soon?"

"You bet."

"Take it easy."

"You too."

Lucy switched over and answered Mandy's call, who, as it turned out, had a quick question about history. After getting off the phone with Mandy, Lucy did a happy dance with Pam, who looked at her as if she was crazy.

Why didn't I think of this whole risk thing earlier?

She hoped she would see Sam online soon. Given that she could actually edit her thoughts, Lucy knew could be more witty and dateable online. The green-eyed brunette began walking back to her house when the sudden reality of the situation came crashing in.

Hold your horses, Luce, you already know this guy is the CAPTAIN of your rival Line. If any of the guys on your Line ever found out, you would NEVER hear the end of it. In fact, knowing them, they will probably kick you off the Line just on principle. It was one thing to think he was cute, but actually dating him?

Hello? Do I need to remind you that for the first time in my life someone asked me out! I mean, *someone* who I've only met *once* asked *me* out.

I guess. It seems like playing with fire.

Well, that's a risk I'm willing to take. Plus, of course, this would never be a problem for any of them. If Tom wanted to date a Majorette from South, the guys would probably think he was a hero or something.

So, what are you going to do?

Lucy's mind started trying to figure out ways around this problem as she walked back to the house and completely forgot about calling Nevada back.

The junior bass drummer was distracted as she walked into the band room on Friday. This was the final practice before school started—before the magic of the summer finally wore off and the reality of classes, tests, quizzes, and projects set in. Lucy knew she could handle the stress, but when her schedule included intense band practices two days a week, games on Friday, drum line sectionals on Wednesday and the possibility of trying to start a relationship with the Captain of the rival drum line, things could get a little chaotic. Molly noticed right away something was up, "Hey Luce, you ok?"

"Yeah, I'm fine. Have you seen Nevada anywhere?"

"I thought I saw him in the percussion room."

"Thanks!"

Feeling embarrassed that she hadn't returned his call yet, Lucy walked in the exact opposite direction of percussion room. She looked over at the Auxiliaries section of the band room to find either Gina or Mandy. Part of her was absolutely bursting to tell them about Sam, but another part wanted to keep the budding romance to herself a little longer. She wasn't sure how they would react. Of course, they would be happy for her, but Lucy didn't want them telling anyone else until she knew exactly what was going on. Fortunately for Lucy, Mandy was bursting with some news of her own. The girls found a somewhat private corner in the crowded room.

"Jerm asked me on a date!"

Gina and Lucy shared a genuine smile. It was no secret that Mandy was a major flirt. She had left a string of broken-hearted guys behind her since they started high school and honestly, this trend had been going on since kindergarten. It was rare to see her get so excited about a guy. Usually boys fell all over themselves in front of the beautiful blond—so she was usually not impressed by the most of the guys she had dated so far. However, this time seemed different, as Mandy was actually excited about the date.

"What are you guys going to do?" asked Gina.

"He mentioned something about going to get ice cream on the first day of school. What do you think I should wear? Do you think I should wear my flowy brown skirt or my light blue sundress with the flowers?"

As Mandy chatted about her wardrobe options, Lucy's head was spinning.

Did all guys everywhere get together and decide the ice cream was the new dinner and a movie? How in the crap am I going to get out of this?

Jerm and Sam were HUGE rivals. Not only in drum line, but in concert band endeavors as well. They were forever battling for the All State title. There was no way that they could miss each other at Scoop It Up. Lucy was going to have to think of a good excuse to give Sam.

"Hey girls—I have to get my drum out. Catch you after practice?"

Her friends nodded and kept discussing the virtues of a cute skirt vs. a cute sundress for Mandy's date with Jerm. Lucy went to the percussion room and pulled out her drum. Fortunately, Nevada had already taken the cymbals outside so she could continue avoiding him. She found her carrier, stand, and music and went out in front of the school to circle up for the Battery warm up. As she walked down the hall, she watched her fellow drummers. They were such a crazy, loyal group.

But where are my loyalties? Can I just throw away the past week at band camp so easily? Isn't this just the excuse the guys are looking for to point out how girls shouldn't be on The Battery?

Who are these guys to say who you can or cannot date? What if Sam is the love of your life? What happened to that resolution?

But is dating Sam taking a risk or potential Line suicide?

Lucy sighed. She had a lot on her mind as Jerm started the warm up.

What about Nevada?

What about him? He's known you for two years and hasn't really given you any 100% definite signals that he *does* have feelings for you.

I know ... I just wish ...

Let's not forget that Sam has at least put forth the effort of asking you out.

Nevada had been watching Lucy all of practice, which was not an easy thing to do considering he had a large pair of cymbals in his face. It was difficult reading her expression behind those dark Oakley sunglasses. She seemed distracted somehow and not at all her usual self. Nevada smiled to himself remembering the previous week. The cute brunette hadn't even been on his radar until just a few weeks ago and he was wondering how he could've missed such a cool chick for the past two years. Nevada had had his share of girlfriends, but they all lacked Lucy's spark and the connection the two of them shared. The second bass drummer was all the things he wanted in a girlfriend—cute, fun, smart and could just as easily hang with the guys as go shopping with the girls. He called her last night because he had missed talking to her like they did at band camp. Nevada crashed and choked his cymbals. He couldn't wait much longer; he was going to make his move after practice.

At the end of a long, sweaty practice Lucy was still no closer to deciding what to do about Sam. She made her way through the crowded percussion room and put her drum away and headed out to her car. Even Mark had noticed how quiet she had been. He had tried repeatedly to push her buttons and get her into a fight, but nothing seemed to get through to his section mate. Lucy had already told Gina and Mandy during one of the breaks that she was going to go home after practice.

Finishing with the cymbals a few minutes later, Nevada looked around the percussion room and didn't see Lucy anywhere.

Tom, who had been picking up the tension between his two friends, winked at Nevada, "She went out to her car just a few minutes ago."

Nevada took a deep breath and rushed out to the parking lot.

Because the Line had practiced an extra half hour, the parking lot was pretty much deserted. Lucy heard someone across the parking lot.

"Wait up, Helena!"

She looked up—only one person would call her that. It was an inside joke that had started last week at band camp. Lucy had joked with Nevada that the only reason he spent time with her was because she was an expert masseuse. He had christened her Helena, as it was the most Swedish name he could come up with.

"Only for you, Sven Petersen."

Lucy had come up with her own name for him. She wheeled around, coming almost face to face with Nevada and those intense hazel eyes of his. It was enough to make any girl swoon. The chemistry and tension that had been between them at band camp suddenly flared up again.

Nevada cleared his throat, "Hey, Lucy ..."

"Oh, hi, Nevada. Sorry I didn't call you back last night. I was completely wiped out from band camp," Lucy said lamely.

"Yeah."

"So, why did you call? Your other masseuse wasn't available?" Lucy asked flirtatiously.

Nevada smiled, "No, she went on strike, actually. The reason I called was, uh, um, to see if maybe you wanted to get some um, coffee some time ..."

Lucy was in utter and total disbelief. First of all, there was the shock of being asked on two dates, two days in a row! Secondly, she had waited so long to hear those words from Nevada's mouth, she was momentarily at a loss for words.

Say yes!!!

Of course I'm going to say yes, but shouldn't I at least mention that I'm also going out with Sam?

Isn't it a little early to make that call?

What do you mean?

Since you technically haven't been out with Sam, there's nothing Nevada actually needs to know about.

Eventually, though, I'll have to tell him.

That's your call. I mean, if you tell him, do you think he'll still want to go out with you?

No. Maybe. I doubt it.

For now, isn't it enough that they go to different schools? And isn't it 'riskier' to date them both at the same time?

Without giving things much further thought, she blurted out, "That sounds great."

A grin broke across Nevada's handsome features, "I was hoping you'd say that."

Lucy wanted to stand for the rest of the evening with her long time crush, but the moment was completely broken by the rest of the Line coming out to the parking lot. Nevada tucked his hands in his pockets and walked away saying, "See you in class on Monday. We'll talk about our coffee sometime next week."

Lucy, now in a Nevada-induced haze, got into her car. She thought she heard music. She *did* hear music—it was coming from her cell phone. Looking at the screen, Lucy was not that surprised to see who had sent her the text message.

>> *Can't wait til Monday. Ice cream Saturday?*

4

BEGINNINGS

Snare drum *n. A tubular drum made of wood or metal with skins, or heads, stretched over the top and bottom openings, and with a set of snares (cords) stretched across the bottom head. This is the lightest drum on the Battery and most often where you will find the Captain of the section.*

At home, Lucy tried to delay her response to Sam by writing in her journal where she penned a very Nevada-centric entry. She sat down to try and do some studying, however, her green eyes seemed to have a mind of their own and kept darting over to the cell phone laying on her bed. She wanted to respond to Sam's invitation, but wasn't exactly sure how to best express herself. Two hours ago, she would have known her exact answer, but then again, that was before Nevada had officially shown interest. Giving up on studying, Lucy went to check her email and maybe do a little chatting with some of her friends. She was secretly hoping that Cartwright213 would be online. They had "met" online Lucy's freshman year and she could still talk to him (at least she hoped it was a him) about all the people in her life with complete honesty. Lucy frowned as she saw he wasn't online. She was about to turn off her computer when an instant message popped up on her screen. It was from *snarejockey1*. She quickly thought through all the drummers she knew. None of them matched the name.

snarejockey1: Pretty please, with Swedish fish on top?

Lucy smiled. Sam was persistent and this little message also solved her dilemma of accidentally running into Jerm and Mandy on Monday.
What exactly are you waiting for?
Isn't this technically cheating on Nevada?
You haven't even gone out with Nevada and already you're giving up on Sam?
Well …

C'mon, he asked so nicely. With Swedish fish on top. Also, because the actuality of Sam and Nevada ever running into each other isn't very good <u>at least</u> until November.

Lucy typed.

bassgirl17: *Sorry I didn't text u back. Was at band practice.*

Not a total lie … I really was at band practice …

snarejockey1: *Me too. The one where I wear the drum, not sit behind it.*
bassgirl17: *Good to know. It must have been one hot practice. It's like a million degrees out today!*

Lucy herself was still gross from her practice earlier today. She was glad that Sam couldn't see through the computer.

snarejockey1: *Yeah. I wouldn't want to be around me right now. How was ur practice?*
bassgirl17: *We're just getting together. So … it's a little rough.*
snarejockey1: *Just give it some time. So, how about tomorrow night?*
bassgirl17: *Fine by me!*
snarejockey1: *That's what I was hoping you'd say. I'll see you around 7?*
bassgirl17: *:) Looking forward to it.*
snarejockey1: *Sweet dreams.*

Lucy signed off and got out her journal again, trying to reconcile her feelings. Having wanted a boyfriend for most of her teenage years and determined to take bigger risks, it was difficult to turn down two offers, even if it meant she wasn't being completely honest. Lucy swore that she would tell them both, eventually …

Between everything that was going on, practice and boys and the start of school, Lucy had some trouble falling asleep that night. She woke up late the next morning with the previous day fresh on her mind. Over a breakfast of banana pancakes, Lucy pondered the burning question of what exactly one wears to eat ice cream with a very cute boy one has just met.

Maybe I should have paid attention to what Gina and Mandy were talking about yesterday.

You could always call and ask their opinion.

And say what, 'Oh by the way, I'm going out with the Captain of South's Line?' I don't think so.

To make the day go faster, Lucy pulled out her studies for AP US History. After what seemed like five minutes, Lucy glanced at the clock and was surprised to see that she had studied for two hours. Walking into the kitchen, Lucy casually mentioned to her Mom that she would be going out "with a friend" that night. She thought she was off the hook until her mother replied, "Who are you going with? Fred? Tom? You and Tom haven't been out in awhile."

"No, Mom. I'm actually going with uh, Sam." Lucy made a move to leave the room, not wanting to answer the inevitable question.

Becky, who wasn't born yesterday, casually asked, "And who is Sam?"

Lucy answered honestly. She couldn't help herself—she was dying to tell someone about this date! She knew that her Mom had liked all the percussionists she had met so far. Lucy said tentatively, "He's a drummer, Mom, and he goes to South."

Becky knew of the huge rivalry between the two schools. They competed at everything: sports, academics, debate, basically, at any time you could have one team vs. another team, South Washington and Forrest Hills were there trying to get the bragging rights.

"South? I take it you haven't introduced your new friend to the rest of the Line?"

"Not exactly."

"Well, maybe you should."

"We're only hanging out. It doesn't necessarily mean anything."

"You know best then. Be home by midnight."

Lucy really did not know best. All she knew was that she was really looking forward to tonight. As much as she wanted to call Mandy and Gina, she still wanted to keep Sam to herself. This fact, however, did not stop her from calling and telling them about her developments with Nevada. Both girls were very excited for her. After getting off the phone, Lucy began tearing through her closet, looking for something that looked like she wasn't trying too hard for a simple evening of ice cream. After countless options, she decided on low-rise khaki shorts with one of her favorite thrift store t-shirts and black and white Puma track shoes. She wasn't going to change her personality for some guy, and a sundress or skirt was definitely not Lucy Karate.

Promptly at seven o'clock, Sam's black PT Cruiser pulled up in front of the Karate household. Lucy, wanting to delay interaction between the South senior and her parents for at another evening, ran out to the car, yelling behind her, "Bye Mom! Bye Dad! Bye Craig! Bye Pam!"

Sam, a little confused, asked, "Who's Pam?"

"My pug."

Sam smiled back at her, "Ok. She could come with us you know."

Lucy liked her date more already. Pam could break any awkward silence or tension. Lucy said, "Let me just run in and get her."

Lucy grabbed a surprised Pam and her leash and ran back out to the car. Sam opened the door for Lucy and Pam. Upon hopping in the car, there was never a lull in conversation and Lucy only felt a small amount of pressure to tell Sam that she really played second bass for the Forrest Hills Flyers Drum Line and that, in a mere three months, they would be competing in a big Indoor competition which would most likely cause him to never want to see her again.

They had been at Scoop It Up for over an hour and the ice cream cones were long gone when Lucy suggested going to the local park, where they could take Pam for a walk. Sam thought it was a great idea. After walking for a while, they settled on the swings.

Lucy asked Sam, "So big senior, do you know where you want to go to school next year?"

He shrugged before answering, "I really don't know. I mean, it seems so far away right now that it's not really a reality."

"You never know, Runaway Truck Ramp could take off and then you'd get to be a drummer professionally."

Sam was silent a moment and looked over at Lucy. He took her smaller hand in his larger, muscular one. Lucy's heart beat a little faster. Sam looked at her intensely, "You know, I can't help feeling that we've met each other before," he said as he traced small designs on her palm.

Lucy gulped. Sam was a smart guy, and he was going to figure things out sooner or later. She racked her brain for another subject. Just then, none other than Murray Meyer walked up. It was the first time Lucy had seen him since the end of school in May. Murray ran on the cross-country team who sometimes practiced at the park. Flushed and sweaty, he had obviously just finished a work-out. Lucy was glad he wasn't wearing anything blatantly Forrest Hills, but realized something with Forrest Hills on it would have been better than not wearing a shirt at all! Lucy noted with interest that the Class Prez must have been working out this summer.

"Hey Lucy!" her classmate said with obvious enthusiasm.

Lucy gulped again. She had wanted a distraction, but she really didn't want another guy to be it.

"Hey Murray." Lucy was unable to return his optimism.

Lucy didn't say anything else, hoping that Murray would get the hint. He clearly did not get that she was on a date. Lucy sighed as he sat down in the next swing. She made awkward introductions between the two. Fortunately, and much to Lucy's delight, Sam chose this moment to act like a boyfriend. He took Lucy's hand and pulled her up, "Nice to meet you, Murray, but we were actually just leaving."

Lucy smiled for a number of reasons. First of all, *take that Murray!* She had liked him ever since they had Biology together and now here she was—cute boy in tow. Second of all, Sam was still holding her hand!

"Come on Pam," Lucy called over to her dog, "Good to see you, Murray!"

It was getting late, so Sam drove Lucy back home. Lucy got out of the car slowly. As she had never been on a real date, she had no idea how to act at this point of the night other than what she had seen on TV and in films. With all her guy friends, she just gave them a hug (Tom got a kiss on the cheek) and went inside. Her heart fluttered nervously, as she didn't know if she should linger or what sort of signs to give Sam as they walked to the door. Lucy was glad for the small miracle that was the side garage door. There was more privacy there than under the blazing lights of her front porch.

Lucy took a deep breath and turned around once they reached the door, ready to tackle Sam with a lame hug. As luck would have it, there was no need for all her concern. As she pretended to fumble with her keys, Sam's strong hand shot out around her waist, pulling her in close. As Lucy held her breath, he leaned in to kiss her as if it was the most natural thing in the world. The kiss started out softly, but their attraction, which had been building since they met at the movie theater, quickly made the kiss much more intense. Lucy was amazed at how the two of them just clicked together. After making out with South's Captain for quite a few minutes, the Forrest Hills second bass stepped breathlessly away before things headed towards actual second base. She looked up at Sam and said with swollen lips, "I have to go. See you soon?"

Sam nodded, smiling, "You can count on that. I'll call you."

Lucy went inside, unable to keep the smile off her face. What a perfect date … and there was only one person in the whole world who she could spill all her feelings to—Cartwright213. She crossed her fingers, hoping that he would be online. He was!

Cartwright213: Were we out enjoying the last of our summer holiday?

Lucy smiled. In the course of their online friendship, she had determined that Cartwright lived somewhere in her general area, was also in high school, and had a pretty decent explanations for the often annoying and confusing behaviors of his gender.

bassgirl17: Yes. I have so much to tell you!
Cartwright213: It's not my fault you've been at band camp.
bassgirl17: I know. So, do you remember me telling you about Nevada?
Cartwright213: Let's see if memory serves me … "a red-headed dream?"
*bassgirl17: *blush* He asked me out!*
Cartwright213: And …?
bassgirl17: It was awesome. But …
Cartwright213: How can there be a 'but'? I thought you liked this guy forever.
bassgirl17: I met another guy.
*Cartwright213: You **have** been busy. *Smirk**
bassgirl17: It's not like that! I don't know who I like better or if I should tell each other about the other.
Cartwright213: Well, if you all go to the same school I'm pretty sure that one's going to work itself out.
bassgirl17: That's just it! They don't!
Cartwright213: Well, the best thing to do is to be honest. 'Cause if you don't, the whole thing is going to blow up in your face.
bassgirl17: Yeah … but Nevada isn't going to be happy when he hears about Sam.
Cartwright213: Who would want to share bassgirl?
bassgirl17: Ha ha, very funny. With me, you know it's more complicated than that.
Cartwright213: How so?
bassgirl17: Sam happens to go to a rival high school, and is on THE rival drum line.

There was a slight hesitation before Cartwright responded. Lucy was too excited to finally share her news with someone to really take notice.

Cartwright213: That definitely changes things.
*bassgirl17: I know. *sigh* I guess I'll let things go for awhile. I've never dated two guys at the same time before. Who am I kidding? I've never dated any guys before.*
Cartwright213: As I've told you before, that's their loss, not yours.
bassgirl17: So, how are things in your life?

Cartwright213: Well, recently they got VERY complicated.
bassgirl17: Do you want to talk about it?
Cartwright213: Not at the moment.
bassgirl17: Fine by me. I'm tired.
Cartwright213: Goodnight then, bassgirl.
bassgirl117: Good night, Cartwright.

Lucy signed off. She always felt better after talking to her online buddy. There was no pressure and now, at least she had been completely honest with ONE person in her life.

The first day of school as an upperclassman at Forrest Hills was a good one for Lucy Karate. As usual, Lucy and her friends collected in the band room before school. It was the unofficial place to cram for a test, catch up with friends you didn't have class with, trade notes, and, if you were dating, a good place to spend some quality time with your boyfriend or girlfriend for those last minutes before the bell rang and you were separated for the day. Lucy looked around, knowing that no one knew she had spent Saturday night with a rival drummer. That knowledge made for an exciting start to her junior year.

Later that day, sitting at the percussion table in the lunchroom, Lucy wondered what Sam was doing right now over at South. Her mind had been drifting towards Saturday night's kiss all weekend. She was wandering into a Sam filled daydream, when she heard Jerm say, "So this year, I think we should take it to the next level. I want to really intimidate South's Line."

Hearing the word 'South,' Lucy perked up and leaned in to pay attention to the conversation.

Doug spoke up, "Like, what do you mean?"

Jerm said off-handedly, "Nothing violent. Maybe a few pranks. Mostly, I was just thinking we find out where they practice and go watch. Let them know that we're not backing down from anything this year."

Adam asked, "You think the whole Line should go?"

Jerm replied, "Nah, just the upperclassmen."

Lucy put her head in her hands; this was *so* not what she needed.

5

FIRST GAME

***The Battery** n. The marching section of a drum line, included, but not limited to snare, bass, and tenor drums, cymbals, and sometimes a marching xylophone. This section is also responsible for playing cadences and providing a solid beat for the rest of the band. Auditions are generally required to be in this section of the Drum Line and it often attracts the more talented percussionists.*

Lucy could only sit and listen as the seniors plotted the most intimidating way to show up the South Washington drum line. The bass drummer knew Jerm would never admit to it, but she suspected it was more of a personal problem he had with Sam than something the entire Line needed to be involved with. It was too early in the season for South to have anything going on with their competitive Indoor stuff, so these plans were based on Jerm's ego more than anything else.

Finally, the lunch bell rang and the drummers got up to start fifth period—officially listed in everyone's schedules as Advanced Percussion Techniques, but really Drum Line 101. Nevada caught up with Lucy as they walked down the hall and tickled her from behind. Lucy was suddenly overcome with a wave of shyness. After liking him for so long, it was like she was in the middle of a dream that someone was going to rudely wake her up from. She tentatively looked up and smiled. Those hazel eyes were just too much.

"So how about Saturday sometime?"

"That sounds great."

Lucy watched as Nevada walked down the hall.

Tell him about Sam!!!

I can't! If I do, he'll never look at me that way again!!

*If you don't, he will **never** look at you again.*

Lucy pondered that dilemma as class went by quickly. As the percussionists put away their instruments before the next bell rang, Jerm barked, "I need to see all upperclassmen after school today! Meet here and don't be late."

Lucy walked out of the band room and on to her next class, alone. She was in her own world walking down the hall when she felt someone take her hand. It was Nevada. Lucy, alone for so long, who had watched Mandy and Gina have countless boys escort them, squeezed Nevada's hand. In the concrete walls of high school, it meant something to have someone hold your hand while walking to class. Especially if that someone was an attractive member of the senior class …

Another point for Nevada. Sam will never be able to do this.

After school, all of the drum line upperclassmen had gathered in the percussion room. Nevada took a seat next to Lucy.

Jerm announced, "So, every year, the competition with South gets more intense. And this year I want to step things up."

Adam said, "Yeah, yeah, you said that at lunch, but how is watching their rehearsal going to accomplish anything?"

The other guys nodded.

Jerm, on the defensive, replied, "Well, I want them to know that we're around, and we're not backing down."

Doug spoke up, "Uh, Jerm, I think they know that already. It's no secret. We've traded first and second with them since anyone can remember."

Jerm, pride wounded, asked, "Well, does anyone have a better idea?"

The room was silent.

If you were looking for one of those 'risk' things, this would be the moment.

Uh, hello? The risk thing was only about the whole romance thing in my life, not every single moment!

Then Lucy, surprising even herself, blurted out, "Infiltration!"

The guys all laughed.

Jerm rolled his eyes, "Lucy, what in the hell are you talking about?"

"Um, Molly or I could date one of the guys on their Line."

Lucy looked over to her fellow female percussionist for help, but Molly shrugged. The strawberry blonde Pit Lieutenant had recently started seeing Nick, a goofy, but adorable Sousa player.

Jerm crossed his arms, "And what exactly would that accomplish?"

I would get to date Sam and none of you would be the wiser …

Lucy started rambling, "Well … um, let's say I started 'fake' dating one of the upperclassmen. We would have access to all their stuff. We could get copies of their music. I could go to their rehearsals without being obvious."

"And what exactly would *that* accomplish?"

Lucy was just getting warmed up, "Well, let's say they do a really complicated lick, and then we could do a similarly complicated lick and then some. Knowing what they had could only benefit us."

Jerm looked skeptical.

Molly, in the spirit of drum line girls sticking up for each other, tried a different approach, "Remember four years ago when Stomp was the big thing?"

Jerm reluctantly said, "Yes "

Molly continued, "*Everyone* did Stomp at the competitions. The big thing would have been to NOT do Stomp."

Jerm saw where she was going.

Nevada spoke up, "Um. *Problemo.* Wouldn't these South guys recognize you?"

Jerm started talking before Lucy had a chance to say anything, "I doubt it. That good-for-nothing Sam and the rest of the Line would probably only remember those who had been on the Battery. I'm not going to settle for second place my senior year."

Lucy asked, "So, we could give it a try?"

Jerm looked around the group. He was the Captain, but he wasn't a total dictator.

Nevada said quietly, "I'd just like to win because we're the best Line."

Others agreed with him. Quite honestly, so did Lucy.

Jerm said, "I'll think about our options. That's all for now. See you guys tomorrow in class. Snares, follow me."

Everyone broke into sectionals. Lance drilled the basses for a while, but to everyone's surprise it wasn't really necessary. The bass line this year really was clicking. They were getting to sound like one massive drum. Fortunately, the cymbals got done around the same time Lucy's section did and she was pleasantly surprised when Nevada offered to walk her to her car.

This is turning out to be the best first day of school ever!

Tell him, tell him, tell him.

I can't! He'll never walk me to my car again.

Nevada didn't say anything when they got to Lucy's car, but leaned in and gave her a soft, quick kiss filled with promises of things to come.

He said softly, "I've wanted to do that all day."

In a rare moment, Lucy had literally been rendered speechless.

Nevada kept grinning and turned to walk to his own car, calling out behind him, "I'll call you later."

Lucy drove home mostly happy but somewhat confused. In addition to Nevada's surprise kiss (which was currently on automatic replay in her mind), she had a lot to consider. If Jerm decided to go ahead with the "infiltration" thing, would she even want to go through with "fake dating" Sam? However, if he decided to go and show up at South's game, Sam would definitely learn the truth of the situation. So, that put a two-week limit on whatever was going on with Sam. Lucy knew there was no way she was going to get out of the prank. It would become legend as the history of the Line went on. Not to mention that being a junior gave her access to this special event. Could she go incognito? In a group of guys, it wouldn't be that difficult to just be one of them. Could Sam even recognize her from a distance? Or in a group? Maybe that was the risk that Lucy would have to take.

When Lucy got home, she got online to check her e-mail. She wasn't surprised when *snarejockey1* popped up on her computer screen.

snarejockey1: How was your first day of school?
bassgirl17: Pretty decent. U?
snarejockey1: Can't complain. It's nice being a senior.
bassgirl17: I can imagine.
snarejockey1: So hey, when can I see you again? :)

Lucy nervously chewed her lip. This Saturday was currently off limits, because she wasn't sure what was going to happen with Nevada. How was she going to get out of this? Her parents were pretty strict when it came to going out on school nights—especially with all the practices she had during the week. Lucy also knew that everyone in any marching band around the world had practice after school Tuesday and Thursday.

bassgirl17: Well, I'm busy Wednesday and I think I'm going to our football game on Friday. How about Tuesday or Thursday?
snarejockey1: Hmmm. No can do. I have band practice and work. How about a late night Friday rendezvous?
bassgirl17: Sounds dangerous. ;)
snarejockey1: Not really. I was thinking donuts.

Lucy smiled to herself. If there was one thing Sam was doing right, it was appealing to her sweet tooth. She could never pass up Krispy Kremes ... especially when their famous 'Hot' sign was on.

bassgirl17: Krispy Kreme on Pleasant Hill around 10:30?
snarejockey1: I'm there.
bassgirl17: Can't wait!
snarejockey1: Me either.

Lucy signed off, wondering what she was getting herself into.

The first week of the school year wound itself to Friday. Lucy was so excited—it was her first night officially marching with The Battery and her second date with Sam! Continuing the tradition that had started freshman year, Lucy went over to get ready with Mandy and Gina before the game. Lucy's routine required a lot less time than the regimented makeup and hair of the Auxiliaries. Still, it was a lot of fun to just hang out after a long week and gossip. Lucy sat patiently while Mandy French-braided her hair. Lucy looked on jealously as her friends donned their flashy and form fitting uniforms. Mandy filled Gina and Lucy in on how things were going with Jerm (good) and Lucy filled the girls in on her week with Nevada (very good). Gina's flirtation with Jonathan, the trumpet transfer student, was also progressing nicely.

Finally, it was time to leave for the game. Since she had seen her name posted on the list in the Spring, Lucy had waited for this night in anticipation. *She* was going to march on the field. *She* was going to the stadium and play cadences. *She* was going to play cheesy songs in the stands. She was on The Battery.

Lucy wished the girls good luck as she walked into the percussion room. Seeing everyone in uniform for the first time always made her laugh. Most of the drummers were on the lean side of muscular and the uniforms, combined with the carriers they wore under them, always made for an interesting upper body look. The school colors actually came together for a decent uniform. Black pants, black shoes, and a green and grey jacket. Captains and Lieutenants wore a silver braid to show their rank. The Line had fought desperately last year to forego the traditional Shako hat and replace it with a black beret. The berets set the Line apart from the band even more than usual. Lucy tucked her brown ponytail into hers and went outside to warm up.

The Line was good and loose as they marched down to the playing field. Lucy grinned at the number of car alarms they set off, knowing it was the bass drums' deep resonating sound that was the cause. At the stadium, nothing about the night let Lucy down. From playing the Star Spangled Banner to jamming in the stands, Lucy enjoyed her first official evening on The Battery. As a mallet player, the only time she'd got to play in the stands was later in the season when she would try and talk upperclassmen out of their instruments for a song or two. The half time show was a little rough, but it was early in the season and there was a lot of time to work things out. Overall, it was a great experience. For an added bonus—their football team won!

With all the excitement of the game, Lucy had almost forgotten that she had a late night date with Sam. After returning her drum to the percussion room, Lucy quickly ducked into the bathroom and rushed to get out of her uniform and into something a little more glam than sweaty shorts and a tank top. As she walked back through the percussion room to get her stuff, she was welcomed with cat-calls and whistling from her section. She laughed and with a smile on her face told them all where they could put it. As she waltzed out of the band room, Nevada caught up with her.

"Where are you headed tonight, smelling so good?" Nevada leaned over Lucy and breathed in over her neck. Lucy had to suppress an involuntary shudder.

I am definitely NOT going out with the Captain of our rival Line!

"Umm, just hanging with some of the girls. Where are you going?" trying to sound as causal as possible.

"WaHo. If you get lonely or anything, come and find me. If not, I will definitely see you tomorrow."

Tomorrow?

You know, your date with Nevada?

Oh yeah.

She finally responded with a convincing smile on her face, "I can't wait."

6

MEETING THE ENEMY

Front Line/Pit/Front Ensemble n. *The stationary percussion ensemble typically placed in front of the football field. Originally, the front ensemble consisted of keyboard percussion and timpani, the marching versions of which are heavy and awkward. On a large drum line, the Pit may also include a group of "Auxiliary" members. These percussionists play any non-mallet instrument. This group is closest in proximity to the Drum Major. They are often told to "listen back" to the beats of the Battery.*

Nevada's attentions got Lucy's mind racing as she drove. Within the space of a week the boy situation in her life had gone from basically nonexistent to out of control.

I know where I want it be, but I'm not sure how to get there.

Let's be honest, you know exactly how to get there. So why don't you?

And lose them both forever? I don't think so!

She wanted Sam and Nevada to know about each other, because, it was only fair. If the situation were reversed, she would certainly want to know if they were dating someone else. She also wanted Sam to know that she was a proud member of Forrest Hills's drum line. Lucy took a deep breath; she was going to have to tell him, tonight, even if it meant the end of their budding relationship. Lucy put on her bravest face, squared her shoulders, and walked into Krispy Kreme.

Lucy's green eyes were instantly drawn to Sam, who was sitting in the far corner booth looking as cute as ever. Then she noticed he wasn't alone.

Sam face lit up when he saw Lucy, then flushed and within moments he was at her side, "Can I see you for a second?"

Sam grabbed Lucy's arm and pulled her away from the group.

"Who are those guys?" Lucy asked looking over Sam's shoulder. Sporting very similar jackets, Lucy had a good idea who they were. The South Washington High School Drum Line.

Lucy was glad that she had taken off her Forrest Hills Drum Line jacket before going in, but seeing those jackets, all of the brave feelings that had been with Lucy in the car suddenly disappeared. It was one thing to tell Sam the truth when it was just the two of them; it was another thing completely to tell him in front of his entire Line.

"Remember how I told you that I was on drum line?" he asked.

"Yes." *Remember how I told you I wasn't on drum line?*

"Well, it's kind of a tradition that I go out with them after a game. I'm the Captain of the Line. I tried to tell them I had a date, but that only made it worse. So, I hope you don't mind."

"Can we ditch them after an hour or so?" Lucy asked, desperately wishing she could ditch them all this very moment.

Sam smiled, "Thanks for understanding."

Better make the best of a bad situation …

If there's one thing I know how to handle, it's high school percussionists.

Clarification, at least those you're NOT romantically involved with …

Thinking quickly, she knew what it would take to get their attention and perhaps even teach them a lesson about the fairer sex in the process. Lucy walked back to the group with Sam, a devious smile on her face.

Sam made introductions, "Guys, this is Lucy. Lucy, this is Flip, Ted, Jeff, Massey, Ken, and Snoopy."

Lucy smiled at all of them. She thought she had seen a girl or two on their Line before, but there were none here tonight. Sam took a seat and she squeezed in next to him. Sam took her hand under the table and squeezed it gently. She saw some of the guys were giving Sam looks of approval around the table. Lucy rolled her eyes, but was secretly flattered. *Boys … nothing ever changes.*

Ted spoke up first, "So, you go to Forrest Hills?"

Lucy said, "Yes. I go to Forrest Hills. So, now we can never talk again, isn't that how it goes?"

Ted laughed, "No, it's cool. We go to practically identical schools. As long as you're not in the marching band, it's ok."

Lucy swallowed and asked hopefully, "What's wrong with being in the band? Isn't that what you guys are all in? Isn't it just one big happy family?"

Ken fielded the question, "Not really. Both schools are in competitive marching bands, just like the football teams are. Also, we're on the drum line, so we're not technically in the marching band."

Lucy understood what the difference was. Being a drummer was an interesting paradox. You were part of the marching band … you were the very heartbeat of it, but you were also a unit unto yourselves. There was a distinct line. Plus, you could look cool playing a drum, which wasn't always possible say, playing the clarinet. People in the school may not know much about the inner workings of the marching band, but they could recognize the drummers separately. Lucy knew all this, but asked, "I guess I don't follow. What's the difference?"

Ken looked puzzled. It was very difficult to explain this dilemma to someone who wasn't on the Line, so he just said, "Never mind."

Flip spoke up, "Anyway, we just have some problems with the members the Forrest Hills Drum Line."

Lucy cocked her head, this was interesting, "Really? Who specifically? Wouldn't it be funny if I had class with them or something?"

Snoopy said, "It's that stupid Captain, Jerm, he's such a tool."

Lucy almost spit out her chocolate milk. It was true, Jerm could be a total tool sometimes, but he was also a great drummer and a true Captain. So she said, "Hmmm, I don't know a Jerm. Maybe he's a senior."

She was getting herself deeper and deeper in trouble. If she ever told Sam that she was on the Forrest Hills Line, this conversation was not going to go over well with him. Lucy decided to play her trump card, "So, I always see the drummers at my school tapping on things constantly. Do you guys do that too?"

Jeff smiled, "They are probably doing cadences and rudiments. That's the great thing about being a drummer—you can practice all the time."

Lucy looked at the group, a completely innocent expression on her face. Lucy may not be the best when it came to sight reading or playing a difficult snare lick, but she had been serious about practicing her rudiments. She also knew that drummers looked for any excuse to show off their skills. *Man, we really are predictable …*

She said innocently, "Can you teach me one? It can't be that hard."

Sam shrugged his shoulders, "Ok. Let's start off with something easy. Jeff, let Lucy borrow your sticks." Sam got out his own pair, "Let's try a paradiddle."

Lucy pretended to struggle with the words, "Para … diddle?"

Sam laughed, "Yeah, I know it sounds funny. You just tap out, Left right left left, Right left right right."

Sam began tapping out the rhythm very slowly on the table. Lucy looked at him strangely, but followed what he was doing. She pretended to stutter at first but then picked up speed, until she was keeping time with Sam who had been picking up speed. The guys around the table looked astonished at Lucy's hands. She stopped and put her sticks down.

She smiled. "That wasn't so hard. Maybe I should try out for our Line next year."

Snoopy was the only one who could talk; he said quietly, "Maybe you should."

Lucy decided to push the envelope a little further, "Do you guys have any girls on your Line?"

Massey said, "We have a few underclasswomen at the moment."

Lucy asked, "Are they any good?"

Jeff said, "For girls? They're okay, I guess."

Something in Lucy snapped. There it was. Guys everywhere, had this thing about girls on their Line. Why couldn't they just, for once, say, yeah, she was a great drummer? Period. End of story. There was always going to be that tag line—for a girl. This went further than the South drum line; this went to how she knew the guys on her own Line looked at her. As a girl first, a drummer second and very proud of both facts, Lucy looked at Sam and said, "Excuse me; I have to get something from my car."

With her personal power song (Tomoyasu Hotei's "Battle Without Honor or Humanity") roaring in her head, Lucy went out to her car, reached in and quickly pulled out her jacket. She had earned this jacket—not as a girl, but as a member of the Forrest Hills Drum Line. Lucy ran her fingers over the best Front Ensemble patch she had earned her freshman year. She looked at the Best Percussion Ensemble patches that she had been a part of so far. She imagined the pins and bars she would receive this season. Lucy put it on and walked back into the Krispy Kreme.

The guys saw a young woman walk up that literally stopped their conversation. In front of their table stood a 16-year-old girl with a black and green jacket and an unpleasant expression on her face. Lucy spoke loud enough so the entire restaurant could hear her, "My name is Lucy Karate. I play bass drum on the Forrest Hills Drum Line. I am a drummer, just like the rest of you. My Line will see yours in November—I hope you guys bring your best licks, 'cause we're sounding awesome this year." As an afterthought, she looked at Sam and added, "I'm sorry, I didn't want it to be like this."

She walked out, willing Sam to follow her so she could give him a better explanation. Lucy was more than a little crushed when she didn't hear Sam coming up behind her.

Well, you earned this. What did you think he was going to do?

Didn't that kiss mean anything to him?

Maybe when he thought he was just kissing some nice girl from Forrest Hills and not The Girl on their Battery. If you want to feel better you can always head over to Waho and see Nevada.

Sorry, I don't think that's going to work. The only thing that will make me feel better is if Sam comes out and I can explain to him what I was thinking.

Lucy turned around slowly, but didn't see the dark haired senior anywhere. She got in her car and drove on autopilot to her house. She didn't really feel like seeing anyone. The guys in her Line probably felt the same about her as the guys in the South Line. Getting ready for bed, she still felt terrible about Sam. Lucy couldn't erase his hurt expression from her mind. Motivated by the overwhelming amount of guilt she was feeling, Lucy typed out an e-mail to Sam.

You know, there's this invention called the telephone ...

So I'm a wuss, so what?

Maybe that's ok. I mean, there's a good chance he won't even pick up when he sees who's calling.

Thanks for reminding me.

To: snarejockey1@SWHS.edu

Sam,

Ha! Ha! You got Punk'd ... I wish you could've seen the expression on your face. It was hilarious.

To: snarejockey1@SWHS.edu

Sam,

Look dude—I'm sorry. Even though we're kind of a modern day Romeo and Juliet, I still want to see you. Do you ever want to talk to me again?

Check the box that most appropriately defines your emotions:
( ) I hate Lucy.
( ) I hate Lucy, but I understand that she did what she had to do.
( ) I secretly still want to see her.
( ) I think Lucy is a young woman who exudes strength and beauty in the face of a male dominated section and would love to escort her on a date sometime in the near future.

To: snarejockey1@SWHS.edu

Sam,

Did I also forget to mention that I'm dating a guy on my own Line and he has no clue about you?

To: snarejockey1@SWHS.edu
From: bassgirl17@FHHS.edu

Dear Sam,

I'm not sure exactly what to say to you. I know that I did a horrible thing by not telling you who I really was. The thing is, I knew you wouldn't want to see me if I did tell you. So it was a weird Catch-22. I'm glad I did go out with you ... you're a great guy and I'm glad we ran into each other that day at the movies.

I wish we could put aside the fact that are our Lines can't stand each other. I'd like to see you again, but I understand if you never want to talk to me. I don't know if I would want to either.

South plays Forrest Hills this year at our school. Then band competitions start. And then in November there is Indoor. So, I guess I will see you around.

With all apparent sincerity,
Lucy

Lucy sent the last draft and felt marginally better. She wasn't sure if Sam would ever respond, but hoped he would talk to her before their Lines eventually met.

The next day, Lucy looked at the gorgeous face with hazel eyes in front of her, trying to concentrate, but her entire being was taken up by the overwhelming desire to run home and check her in-box to see if Sam had responded.

You're not being fair ...

I know.

*And must I remind you that this is **Nevada Petersen** sitting in front of you?*

Lucy cringed to herself, realizing how much she must be seriously pissing off the dating gods. She had begged for Nevada to look in her direction and now that he was doing exactly that, she wasn't giving him her full attention. Or even half her attention. Lucy interrupted the cymbal Lieutenant, "Nevada, I'm not feeling well."

He looked momentarily taken back, "Really?"

Lucy nodded sheepishly, "I just really wanted to see you, but with everything that's coming up, I don't want to risk getting sick. Is that okay?"

Nevada flashed a quick smile, "Sure thing, Luce. We'll get you home."

As they pulled up to the Karate residence, Lucy quickly kissed Nevada's cheek and said, "Thanks for understanding."

"You still owe me a date, Lucy Karate."

When he said her name in that tone of voice, it took everything in Lucy's system not to jump back in the car and finish the date. She smiled at the cymbal player, "I know."

As she carefully closed the car door and Nevada watched her walk inside, he mused out loud, "So, she wants to play hard to get?"

As soon as she saw Nevada drive away, Lucy sprinted to her computer and looked to see if she had any new e-mails. When she saw that there were none, tears of frustration began forming and finding their way down her face.

I ended my date early for nothing.

"… in conclusion, I think it would be best if the upperclassmen check them out this Friday. I just don't want them to forget we're around," said Jerm, addressing the upperclassmen gathered at the lunch table.

Lucy breathed a huge sigh of relief. After the dramatics of Friday night, she wasn't going to be able to follow through with her infiltration plan anyway. Then the reality of the situation began to sink in. She was going to see Sam. This Friday.

You could always not show up.

And miss becoming part of a Line legend? I don't think so!

7

LET THE GAMES BEGIN

Cymbals n. Traditionally used in pairs, each one having a strap set in the bell of the cymbal by which they are held. Crashed together, the cymbal produces a loud, sharp, but comparatively short-duration "crash" used mainly as an occasional accent effect, and are most usually 16–19 inches in diameter. Sometimes, during a marching performance, many cymbalists will act as a "ride cymbal" for the snare drummers, to produce a sound like a traditional drum set.

The week wound down to Friday and Lucy *still* hadn't gotten a response of any kind from Sam—not an e-mail or instant message, phone call or text message. The Forrest Hills junior grudgingly got ready for the big showdown between the Lines. She didn't know exactly what was appropriate to wear to see one's opposing drum line that also included a guy you had lied to, but still kind of wanted to date. After penning a series of somewhat depressing journal entries, Lucy realized she was having a harder time than she thought getting over a relationship that had really just started. She also struggled over whether or not to come clean with her own Line, including Nevada, about the whole thing. As her first attempt with the truth hadn't gone so well, Lucy decided against it. Anyway, tonight she planned to hang back and work on being invisible, keeping as low a profile as possible.

Maybe the South drummers have already forgotten that I completely betrayed their Captain …

And Chuck Norris might lose a fight. Face it, it's not going to happen.

After calling Molly to check her wardrobe selection, Lucy opted for black shorts, a green tank top, her drum line jacket, and a visor for optimum blending in. It wasn't dressed up, but no one would mistake her for a guy by the length of her shorts. Lucy smiled at her reflection—she had a great pair of legs and was proud to use them when the situation called for it.

Lucy drove over to the school trying to block out the bad feelings she had about this evening. The upperclassmen quickly assembled. With everyone wearing their drum line jackets, they looked like some sort of weird gang. Finally, the last person pulled up and Jerm gave the ok to head over to the South Washington stadium. Lucy chose to ride over with Molly in Tom's minivan. It took awhile for everyone to get over to South and into the stands. Like Forrest Hills, South Washington's football team was very competitive and usually filled the stands to a capacity crowd.

It was a warm evening early in the fall, the perfect night for a football game, or a halftime show. Jerm had decided that the Line was going to make their move when the South percussionists warmed up at the end of the second quarter. Until then, everyone hung out on the opposing side. South's stands were packed, and wearing a Forrest Hills jacket in the middle of them wasn't exactly the safest option.

As the buzzer sounded, it was time to move. Lucy looked across the field and saw the South drummers making their way down through the stands to warm up, zeroing in on Sam, who was one of the few people who could actually pull off looking good in a band uniform. Nevada grabbed Lucy's hand as they walked over to the South percussionists. Usually, Lucy wouldn't have minded as this display of affection, but she was quick to drop Nevada's hand as they neared South's side. The South Line warmed up like every other drum line, in a half circle with quints on one end, snares in the middle, and basses on the other end. The cymbals hung out in back and stretched out. This setup left optimum room for an Instructor to stand in the middle and hear the Line altogether or for another Line to stare down the opposing drummers. Jerm had chosen the latter of the two. As the Forrest Hills percussionists looked on glaring, the South Line stoically kept their composure as they warmed up.

The night would have gone on in this drama-free standoff if not for one particular event. At the end of the drum solo, the South snares attempted a stick toss from one side of the section to the other. It didn't work and somehow the missing drumstick landed directly in front of Lucy's flip flopped feet. She had a quick, but important decision to make: a) not to do anything b) throw the stick even further away c) try the patented "bend and snap" move from *Legally Blonde*, or d) return the stick to Sam, who was apparently missing one.

Lucy knew she had to do the right thing. It was as if time stood still. Both lines were waiting for her reaction. Lucy calmly bent over, retrieved the ProMark "Fitz Stick," and walked over to Sam. She handed the piece of wood across to him, but not before catching his eye. She mouthed the words, "I'm sorry," hoping he would recognize her apology.

Sam gave her a curt nod.

At least he acknowledged me ... it's a start!

Lucy turned to walk back to her Line. She was almost back to her original spot when someone on the South line said in a low voice, "Bitch."

Lucy understood what that "bitch" meant, but the rest of her Line didn't. Nevada started turning as red as his hair. The rest of the guys looked like they wanted to kill someone. It was one thing to insult the guys on the line or sloppy playing; it was another thing entirely to insult one of their girls.

Nevada spoke up, "That's my girlfriend you're calling a bitch, punk."

This was news for everyone, including one very surprised Lucy. Most of the guys on the Forrest Hills Line had known that Lucy and Nevada had been flirting a little more than usual, but they weren't aware it actually had progressed to a label just yet. Lucy was happy with Nevada, but as they actually had only been on one official date, she thought it was a little preemptive to be throwing out the big "G" word. Sam's blue eyes locked on Lucy's green ones. She shook her head briefly and shrugged at the same time, trying to send the message, *I am sort of seeing him, but still interested in you too and I'm still really sorry for what happened on Friday.*

At this point, things could go either way. The competition between the Lines was a powder keg that had been looking for a catalyst to set it off for a while. Lucy had a vision of an all out brawl, which would be difficult considering the South line were wearing their carriers, uniforms, and drums. Fortunately, cooler minds prevailed. This was all Jerm really wanted anyway—something to charge his Line for the upcoming competitions. Sam, while in uniform, didn't feel like getting almost forty people in a fight. He'd have detention for the rest of his life, not to mention significantly reduce the chances that his Line would get to go to the Indoor competitions in November.

Jerm raised up his hand like he was ending a cadence, "Come on guys. We may have a 'bitch' on our line, but at least she can play."

He turned to leave. The rest of the Line followed.

Lucy rolled her eyes, but smiled at the backwards compliment. As she walked away, she stole one more glance of Sam, wishing that things had worked out differently with the handsome South Washington Drum Line Captain.

The guys didn't stay to see South's halftime show. They would see it in a few weeks at the first band competition and had already seen the percussion portion of it during warm ups. Everyone rode back to the school in a caravan. All anyone could talk about was the "bitch" comment. Lucy knew it was only going to get worse when they told the underclassmen on Monday. The story would become embellished and she knew Jerm would do nothing to stop it.

Back at Forrest Hills, Lucy had to get away from the Line. She was impressed and flattered by everyone's loyalty, but had a sinking suspicion that they probably would have called her the same thing if the situation was reversed. Not pausing to see if Nevada was looking for her, Lucy jumped in her car and started driving. Before long, she found that she had driven herself to where she and Sam had shared their first (and only) date. She parked the car and moodily walked over to the swings.

"I thought I might find you here."

Lucy recognized the voice and promptly fell out of the swing. She was totally embarrassed when Sam extended a strong hand to pick Lucy up. She was glad it was dark out so that he couldn't see how red her face was. Sam took a seat in an adjacent swing.

"I wanted you to know that it wasn't me tonight."

Lucy thought a moment before saying, "I know. I knew it wasn't your voice, but your guys were sticking up for you. They're acting like any good Line should for their Captain."

They swung in silence.

What do I do now?!?!?

Sorry, this particular scenario isn't in the manual; you're going to have to wing it.

Can you give me any advice?

Tell the truth.

Sam's husky voice interrupted her thoughts, "You know what?"

"What's that?"

"You're a pretty gutsy girl."

Lucy smiled at the awkward compliment, "How do you figure?"

"Well, meeting my whole Line like that and then telling them who you really were. Then, coming tonight ... you didn't have to, but you did."

"I had planned on telling you the truth as soon as I walked into Krispy Kreme."

"But you didn't plan on everyone being there?"

Lucy got up and started pacing, "No. I felt terrible every time I saw you or talked to you. I knew that you thought I was someone else, but here's the thing: I am REALLY proud of my spot on the Line. I worked hard for it and have to work harder than everyone else to overcome the whole 'girl' stigma."

"You should be proud of yourself. You're on a really good Line and you can't just be given a spot on Forrest's Battery."

"Thanks. Anyway, I want you to know that I'm not the person who usually lies to people, but when I saw that you were probably never going to talk to me that day at the theater, I got desperate."

Sam laughed out loud.

"What are you laughing at?" Lucy asked, offended.

"I'm just laughing because girls have done some strange things to get my attention, but lying about being on Drum Line may be among the strangest."

Lucy smiled, "I can just picture you at band camp. You must make those little Auxiliary girls giggle like crazy. I know what my boys go through. Don't get me wrong, they love it, but it's not anything they want to pursue."

Sam stopped swinging and looked at Lucy, "My boys? Lucy, my dear, is there something else you are not telling me?"

"My boys as in 'my boyz'? I know you've had girls on your Line, so can't pretend you don't know what I'm talking about, but you don't know the first thing about what's it's like to be a drum line girl. I look at all these girls trying to get my section's attention and think; you don't really know these guys like I do. You weren't there on a freezing Saturday in November when we got 2nd place. You weren't there every day in class to see them. You weren't there to hold their hand when a girlfriend broke their heart. You weren't there on the bus to give them a back massage. You don't know the music or the inside jokes or the first thing about these guys."

"I guess you feel pretty strongly about that."

"You're damn straight I do. These guys are like my brothers—sure, we have a very messed up relationship, but I would do just about anything for them."

"Does that include your 'boyfriend' from earlier tonight?"

Lucy was quiet for a moment, "Oh, um … that's Nevada."

Sam raised his eyebrows, "That seems to be a little bit more than brotherly love."

"Well, about the same time I started seeing you, Nevada and I started a little something."

"Another thing you were planning on telling me?"

Since you're probably never going to talk to me again after tonight, why stop now?

"Yes, actually. Besides, you and I were never exclusive, just like Nevada and I aren't."

"I think that might come as somewhat of a shock to him."

Lucy sighed, Sam was right, but she didn't like talking about Nevada with Sam, so she asked, "So, why did you come here tonight?"

Sam took a minute to answer, "You're not like any girl I've ever met, Lucy Karate. You have a crazy dog, beautiful eyes, and I probably should have guessed that you are a drummer. I love kissing you and you're fun to be around."

Lucy wasn't sure what to say.

"I don't know why, but even after everything I still really want to see you again."

"Well, that makes two of us," Lucy said shyly.

Sam smiled, "Get over here."

Lucy got up and sat down on Sam's lap. She liked kissing Sam too. Lucy asked, "So, what do we do now?"

Sam said, "We see each other very, very carefully. Neither of our Lines can know what's going on. But, you have to promise that you will tell Nevada that you are dating someone else."

"I will," she looked up at him, "A kiss for good luck?"

"Sure thing—we're going to need a lot of it."

Lucy got in her car, and resolved to never lie again. She had a not so fun conversation with Nevada ahead of her.

8

AWAY GAME!

Cadence n. A work played exclusively by the percussion section of a modern marching band, descended from early military marches, primarily as a purposefully emphasized means of providing a beat to marchers. Often times, cadences will have names (i.e. inside jokes) that only make sense to those who play them.

Rather than immediately tell Nevada the truth, Lucy did her best to avoid him the following week. She didn't like doing it, but there hadn't been a good time yet to tell him what was really going on.

That's a lie and you know it.

Fine, but what do you want me to tell him?

You had no trouble telling Sam.

So, I just go up and say, "Oh, by the way, thought you should know, I'm dating Sam, the Captain of our rival Line."

In not so many words …

Since "the incident" the previous Friday, everyone on her Line was pretty convinced it was Sam who had called her a bitch and there was nothing Lucy could say to convince them otherwise. Most of the guys were ready to go over to South and kick some ass.

Lucy was absolutely bursting to tell someone what was really going on. She couldn't tell Gina and Mandy because she wasn't sure they wouldn't understand. Plus, Mandy and Jerm were pretty much together any spare time they had, so there was a good chance Jerm would find out if she did tell the girls. She debated telling Tom and Molly, but was afraid of the fallout it might produce.

Just think, the longer you wait to tell everyone, the worse it will be.

I have to tell someone.

Lucy decided the next chance she got, she would lay it all out for Cartwright213.

The football game that week was outside of the normal county conference. Lucy was a big fan of away games and bus rides. It was some of her favorite quality time spent with the Line. Since her freshman year, her seatmate was usually Tom, but with the whole Nevada thing going on, Lucy wasn't surprised to see that the redhead had saved her a seat near the back of the bus. She thought she had been always dreaming of this day … how nice it would be to have someone special to sit next too, but part of her wondered who Sam was sitting next to on his bus.

Bus #5 was the drum line bus, pure and simple. Having the Line, or at least a good part of The Battery, on one bus worked out better for when they went to competitions and parades. Some of the Auxiliary girls always tried to get on, but unless they had been dating a drum line guy for over a year, they rarely got the privilege. With the Jerm romance, Mandy, along with Gina, had opted for the Bus #5 and for that, Lucy was grateful. Sometimes the bass drummer felt like she missed out on what the rest of her band friends were doing, but then she would look around the bus and not want to be anywhere else.

She took a seat next to Nevada. Everyone was in their "casual uniform." This meant khaki shorts, this year's band t-shirt, and for most of the bus, flip flops, Chuck Taylors, Vans, or some sort of soccer shoe. The black shoes and socks would come out later when everyone changed into their uniforms.

Roll was called. The bus got moving. Everyone got out their sticks and practice pads. If any Lieutenant felt their section needed extra practice, they could do so on the bus. Mostly it was just underclassmen running through cadences, exercises, and rudiments. Going to a game was always completely different than the return trip. Secret conversations, stolen kisses … you never knew what would happen on those long, quiet rides back.

The bus ride to the game was pretty standard. Lucy chatted over the seat with Molly while Nevada drummed with some of the other guys. The game was also uneventful. Their team won. The half time show was the best yet. The other band was considerably smaller and watched in awe as the Forrest Hills High School Marching Band performed. Everyone was in a great mood as they got back on the bus. Lucy spaced for a moment in the middle of all the commotion. She stared out the window and wondered what Sam was doing that very moment. From her backpack, she heard her phone beep. While everyone was getting out of their uniforms, Lucy slyly checked her text message. It was from Sam!

>> *Miss u. Swings 2nite?*

Lucy typed back quickly. >> *Late return. Call u 2morrow?*

>> *:(*

>> *Sorry. Miss u 2.*

Lucy shut her phone and put it back in her backpack. The bus got going and made its way through the dark night. Nevada slid down in the seat next to Lucy. They arranged themselves so Nevada was holding Lucy in his arms. He said quietly, "I feel like I haven't seen you all week."

"I know."

Come on Lucy, it's like Nike says, 'just do it.'

Lucy took a deep breath and trying to keep her voice upbeat and cheery said, "So Nevada, there's something I need to tell you."

"That doesn't sound good."

"Ummm. Well, I guess we've never really talked specifically about our relationship."

"No. Why, should we?"

Here goes nothing. "Well, the thing is, I really like dating you, but you should know that I'm ... well, I'm, um, sort of seeing someone else."

Nevada didn't respond and Lucy felt his entire body tense up. She gulped, this was going so much worse than she could have imagined. She was glad to have got those words out, but it didn't make them sound any better.

Lucy continued, "You don't know him. It just kind of happened suddenly. Like we did, actually. Anyway, he goes to South."

Nevada still didn't say anything. Lucy let out a frustrated sigh. Nevada's silent treatment was not helping the situation.

"Anyway, I want to see you. I like being with you, but if you don't want to date me because I'm dating someone else, I completely understand."

Nevada looked off in the distance away from Lucy. The bass drummer sighed again loudly and said, "So, you think about this and maybe we'll talk this weekend?"

The cymbal Lieutenant mumbled something to the affirmative. Lucy knew he needed some space, so with one more apologetic look back at Nevada; she got up and headed to the middle of the bus. Luckily, Tom wasn't sitting with anyone. She gave him a look and he immediately let her in the seat. She slid down and sighed.

Tom asked, "Trouble with a certain cymbal player?"

Lucy nodded, "However, I don't want to talk about it. How are things with Eight Cadet these days?"

If there was something Tom enjoyed discussing, it was his band. Tom and Lucy chatted the entire ride back to the school. Lucy was glad for the distraction. By the end of the trip, Lucy already had plans to go and see Eight Cadet the following Saturday. They were playing at a local all ages club. It was one of the unwritten rules of having friends in a band; you went to see them whenever they had a show.

The bus pulled up to Forrest Hills around midnight. Lucy got off the bus and walked to the truck. She waited for her bass drum to be unloaded and carried it to the percussion room. She didn't wait for anyone as she walked out to her car. Nevada hadn't so much as tried to catch her eye for the rest of the bus ride home, so she assumed it was a lost cause. Digging through her garment bag and back-pack, Lucy let out a frustrated sigh as she looked for her keys for what seemed like ten minutes.

Damnit! Where the hell are they?

Lucy was surprised when she sensed tears of frustration pricking her eyes.

They're just keys!

"You always keep them in your beret."

Lucy didn't have to turn around to know who was talking to her. She slowly dug out her beret and looked inside, instantly seeing the flash of her key ring. Lucy started to say something, but Nevada brought his finger up to her lips, "Let me talk."

Nevada looked at Lucy with those beautiful hazel eyes of his and Lucy was quiet, "I'm sorry for the way I acted earlier. I'm usually the one who, well, never mind. Anyway Lucy, I don't really want to share you with anyone, but I'm not giving up without a fight."

Lucy looked up at Nevada, "So, we can give this a try?"

Nevada nodded, "Yes, but just know that I'm the one taking you to Home-coming."

Lucy said shyly, "I'd like that."

With that, Nevada reached across and cupped Lucy's chin with his hand, bringing her in for a sweet kiss. Lucy didn't realize how long they had been kiss ing until they heard the catcalls and whistles of the Line walking past them in the parking lot. She blushed, "I'd better go."

"See you later," Nevada said huskily.

9

COMPETITION

Drum Corps/DCI *n. A musical marching unit (similar to a marching band) consisting of brass instruments, percussion instruments, and color guard. Typically operating as independent non-profit organizations, drum corps perform in field competitions, parades, and other civic functions. The prime age for participation is 14–22. Many high school wind and percussion players strive to be members of these elite groups.*

Lucy drove away from the school wondering what was wrong with her. The easy answer was staring her in the face. Dump Sam, date Nevada. It seemed like last Spring all she had wanted to do was make The Battery and date a nice boy. Now, she was marching second bass and dating two boys at the same time. Was it time to bring in Mandy and Gina? Lucy pondered this question. It was still too risky. If she told Gina, then Mandy would probably find out and most likely Jerm would hear about Sam and Lucy and then … Lucy shuddered. It wouldn't be pretty. Lucy had already had nightmares about the Line finding out. She could picture Nevada's angry face and she didn't want to be the cause of it.

Why didn't I just tell him tonight?

Because then you wouldn't have such a cute date to Homecoming.

That can't be the only reason.

Would you feel better if you told Tom or Molly?

Hello? That would be a total mistake. Maybe before the whole 'bitch' thing, but now? It's too late.

Lucy decided an unbiased opinion was the one she needed. She signed online, desperately hoping that her old buddy would be around. There he was! Lucy began typing frantically.

bassgirl17*: AAAAAAAAHHHHHHHHH!*
Cartwright213*: What seems to be the trouble, ma'am?*
bassgirl17*: I have gotten myself into a bad situation.*

Cartwright213: Do tell, young grasshopper.
bassgirl17: V. Funny. So remember those two guys I was telling you about?
Cartwright213: Yes. Please tell me you've managed to inform them about each other.
bassgirl17: Well, that's half true …
Cartwright213: You've only told one? Well, I guess that's a good start.
bassgirl17: See, that's the thing, I can't really tell the other one.
Cartwright213: And why is that?
bassgirl17: Ummm. Well, you know how Clark Kent is really Superman?
Cartwright213: You're dating a superhero?!
bassgirl17: No. So, Guy #1 knows I'm dating Guy #2, and Guy #2 knows I'm dating someone else, but if Guy #2 knows the real identity of Guy #1, then I'm totally screwed!
Cartwright213: Come on, it can't be that bad.
bassgirl17: Yes, it actually can. Think of the person you hate more than anyone.
Cartwright213: Ok, got it.
bassgirl117: What? No name?
Cartwright213: I don't want to say. Maybe you know him.

Lucy leaned back from her computer and thought a moment. Two years ago, she had entertained the romantic idea that she might actually know Cartwright in real life. When they had first started chatting, they had both agreed to keep things as "impersonal" as possible, so they only knew that they lived in the same county, were both in high school, and vague physical descriptions, but nothing further.

bassgirl17: Ok, Mr. Secretive. So, pretend you were dating someone. You knew she was dating someone else, but she wouldn't let you know exactly who it was, and that was because she was dating your worst enemy.

Cartwright was silent for a minute.

bassgirl17: Hello? Answer please.
Cartwright213: Ok, I get what you're saying. You're between the proverbial "rock and a hard place." Do you really like them each that much? Why not just pick one and get it over with? The longer it goes on, the worse it's going to be.
bassgirl17: I know. But I really do like them both that much.
Cartwright213: I don't think that's possible. I think if you really thought about it, you would be able to pick one over the other.

bassgirl17: *Maybe …*
Cartwright213: *Women …*
bassgirl17: *C'mon Cartwright, let me live a little. Who knows when this will happen again? This is me we're talking about.*
Cartwright213: *If word gets out of what you have done, it might be awhile before any guy wants to go near you again.*
bassgirl17: *(pouting)*
Cartwright213: *I know it's not what you want to hear, but it's the truth. Think about how this is all going to end.*

Lucy played with her hair nervously before responding.

bassgirl17: *At the end of the season, nobody's the wiser? I join an exclusive club for girls who've dated two hot guys and lived to tell.*
Cartwright213: *Do you think this is some sort of lame after school special?*
bassgirl17: *No.*
Cartwright213: *Then tell the truth! If neither of them wants to stay with you, then that's what you deserve. If one of them wants to be with you after all the cards are on the table, then you've found yourself a winner …*

Lucy signed off and closed her computer and got into bed, feeling only marginally better that someone else knew what was really going on, but unhappy with her anonymous friend's recommendations.

What does he know anyway? It's not like he's had to watch his best friends constantly date people for the past two years.

He does know about your past. Whether you want to believe it or not, he IS looking out for your future. Do you think Gina and Mandy would tell you any differently?

Lucy knew what the answer to that would be and pushed it to the back of her mind.

Lucy's schedule fell into a steady rhythm. Over the next couple of weeks, at school and practices, she enjoyed the romantic attentions of Nevada and hanging with the Line. On the weekends and rare weekday nights, she got to hang out with Sam. Her time with Sam seemed intensified, but she guessed that was most likely due to the fact that their time together was limited. On one such evening in early October, Lucy sat encircled in Sam's arms. They were watching a movie. Ok, "watching" was a relative term. They hadn't seen each other all week and had to make up for the lack of time. Lucy broke a kiss with Sam and looked up at him, "You know it's not going to be pretty if we see each other at the competition this weekend."

to make up for the lack of time. Lucy broke a kiss with Sam and looked up at him, "You know it's not going to be pretty if we see each other at the competition this weekend."

"No, it's not."

"I'll be there with Nevada. Everyone in the band knows we're dating."

Sam sighed, "Well, there's no way that I'm going to be able to make that claim." Lucy asked flirtatiously, "Want to make tomorrow even more interesting?"

Sam looked at her, "Whatever could you be talking about, Ms. Karate?"

Lucy laughed, "The competition, of course."

Sam nodded, "A wager then, on whose Line is going to capture the High Percussion caption?"

"Yes. If I win, then I get to go to your Homecoming." Lucy carefully watched Sam's reaction to her proposition, wondering if she should be committed for her complete lapse in mental judgment, but he appeared to actually be considering it.

He replied smoothly, "What if I told you I was already planning on asking you anyway?"

Lucy looked at him, shock clearly written on her face.

This can only end badly ...

Stop being such a pessimist! Two Homecomings with two different guys?! What's not to like?

You're going to have to listen to me eventually ...

"Well? Will you go with me?" Sam whispered in her ear.

"I'd love to," Lucy replied, quashing any guilty thoughts.

The next day, Henry passed out the eagerly anticipated music for the upcoming Indoor Drum Line competitions. The theme of this year's show included selections from Green Day's *American Idiot* album. While the rest of the band was concentrating and working on the halftime show for competition, the Line had double duty—practicing their old music and drill *and* learning the new music and drill for November.

Lucy pulled out her calendar during Pre-Calc and gulped. As of this weekend, first semester really took off. The upcoming Saturday was the first band competition. She knew that Sam and his Line would be there. It would be the first time the lines had seen each other since the "Bitch" incident. The weekend after that was another competition, where they would also both be attending. The weekend after that was Forrest Hills's Homecoming and the weekend after that was

South's Homecoming. Then came the first of two Indoor Competitions! Lucy could only hope she would come out of this semester alive.

Jerm called for everyone's attention, before class started, "Alright guys. Tomorrow is the first big test. Y'all know that South is going to be there. I don't want anyone getting kicked out or in trouble before the competition starts. I need all of you ready to drum your asses off. Let's show some class—we're the Forrest Hills Drum line, after all. We'll show them on field."

Nevada looked at Lucy and whispered, "I'll protect you."

Jerm was finishing up, "So, I'll see everyone here tomorrow morning! Don't even think about being late."

There was nothing like the first band competition of the year. Freshman wandered around in a daze, wondering if they would be the ones to mess up, fall out of step, play a wrong note and lose it for the entire band. The seniors walked around secretly worried as well. These competitions were their legacies. There was nothing worse than knowing that you were going to graduate with a second place trophy for your final show.

Lucy walked up to Fred, who was pacing up and down the hall. As one of the Drum Majors, Fred was one of the most visible and important members of the band. Lucy gave him a big hug, "You're going to do awesome."

"Thanks, Luce—wish I felt the same way."

"You know you are, and there's nothing more to it. Just listen back to the Battery—we won't let you get off beat."

Lucy walked into the band room. It was chaos. Uniforms, bags, cases, candy, sodas, and secret pal gifts were littered everywhere. Multiple iPods were hooked up to speakers and a range of songs were competing to be the loudest. Mr. Izzo called for everyone's attention and gave his usual speech about teamwork and hard work and then it was time to board the buses.

The bus ride to the competition was a continuation of the chaos. Everyone was hyped up for the day. This was no football game. This was a big competition with bands from all over the state. There were a lot of bragging rights on the table. Once the band had registered, everyone was free to do what they wanted to until warm ups in the evening. As one of the last bands to perform, Forrest Hills could watch most of the other bands or go and intimidate the other drum lines. They usually chose to do the latter of the two.

As they walked around, Lucy was hyperaware that she could run into Sam at any moment. Although she usually enjoyed holding Nevada's hand, she didn't want Sam to …

Sam to what? Get the wrong idea? I think it's Nevada you should be worrying about.

At that exact moment, Sam and some members of the South drum line turned the corner. Lucy took a deep breath, not sure what was going to happen.

Nothing happened.

The South percussionists stared down Nevada and Lucy, but they didn't say anything. Nevada had stared right back, glaring daggers and squeezing Lucy's hand. Lucy looked at the ground and anywhere but at Sam. After the Line had passed them, Lucy looked at Nevada, "I have to go to the bathroom, I'll be right back."

Lucy ducked into the bathroom. That was too close. She got out her phone and quickly texted Sam.

>> *Didn't say it would b ez.* ☺

Within a minute, she got a response.

>> *Wish I was the one holding ur hand.*

She typed back.

>> *May the best line win. ;)*

>> *See u tomorrow nite.*

Lucy smiled. Sam and Lucy had agreed to meet the following afternoon so they could go over what had happened the day before—win or lose.

10

BEST PERCUSSION ENSEMBLE

Drum Major n. *The drum major position is one of leadership, instruction, and group representation. The drum major is responsible for providing commands (verbally, through hand gestures, or with whistle commands or alternatively with a signal baton) to the ensemble regarding where to march, what to play, and what time to keep. A drum major can come to hold that position by either auditioning or being appointed. Some bands may have more than one and even field conductors if the marching unit is large enough.*

After the non-face off with the South Line, the afternoon went by quickly and soon it was time to warm up. Lucy and Nevada went to find the instrument truck. Lucy quickly got into her uniform and nervously got out her drum.

Henry had them line up in the traditional half circle, while an audience gathered. They had a great warm up while Henry tuned their drums. After everyone was good and loose, Henry called for the traditional pre-competition cadence. "The Moon Rules #1" always got everyone in a good mood. The audience, who had been watching, started tapping that feet and moving to the groovy cadence. Lucy smiled. These beats got everyone within a 20-foot radius moving.

Before she realized it, Lucy was gathering with the rest of the band to go down to the field and perform. They lined up to walk out on the field and Lucy felt a surge of pride as she glimpsed the glittery Gina and Mandy with perfect smiles on their faces. Up until now, Lucy always warmed up separately with the Pit and had always been on the field already, waiting for the band. Lucy tried to control the out of control butterflies in her stomach as the band—250 strong—marched out on the field. The green-eyed brunette offered up a quick prayer to whatever marching gods may be listening that she played a perfect show. From the grandstands, a cheer went up and goosebumps shot down Lucy's arms. Forrest Hills's band always did an outstanding job and everyone was looking forward to their show. The Marching Flyers didn't disappoint.

Fred and Elena, the senior FHHS Drum Major, called the band to attention. The band members responded with a resounding and overwhelming "HUT!" while the members of the drum line hit their drums in unison. The cymbals crashed and choked their cymbals at the same time. Overall, it was a huge sound. The crowd cheered appreciatively. Fred and Elena gave their salute and Elena marched quickly to the drum major stand. She climbed it, brought her hands up, and the show began.

Lucy couldn't think about anything else once the performance started. She didn't think about Sam or Nevada or who was going to win, she just thought about her drum and the Line and soon enough it was the drum break. Marching through the solo, Lucy knew the judges had to be impressed. Many drum lines just parked themselves and played through their drum solo. Not the percussionists who wanted the coveted High Percussion trophy. Their drum instructors wrote out drill to march while they were playing some very complicated licks. Forrest Hills was no exception. It seemed like Lucy blinked and the solo was over—a roar of approval went up through the stands. The percussion judge had to move quickly to keep up with them.

The rest of the show was a breeze after the drum solo. On this warm October evening, there was no place else Lucy would rather be. The band marched off, not with a cadence, but with a simple drumbeat. The band collected on the track off the field. Since they were the second to last band to perform and there was no room in the stands anyways, they would just wait patiently until the awards were given out. The Line carefully put their instruments down and waited while the South Washington Band marched on the field.

The South band got a similar reaction as Forrest Hills for their "Hut!" After the Drum Majors signified they were ready to take the field for competition, their show began. Everyone in the Forrest Hills band critically watched South's performance. The scores were going to be very close. Both bands had a high level of difficulty. It seemed that both got an equal round of applause from the crowd. Lucy watched with pride as Sam kept the beat for the band as they marched off the field.

That's my boyfriend out there!

Get it together, Lucy. This guy is on the opposing Line. Do you actually want him to win?

Of course not, but can't a girl be proud of her boyfriend?

The South band lined up next to the Forrest Hills band. All anyone could do now was wait. Fortunately, they did not have to wait long.

An announcement came over the loudspeaker, "Would representatives of the competing marching bands kindly take the field?"

The Drum Majors, Captains, and Lieutenants from each section took the field. For some bands this was a small gathering—maybe five people. For the Forrest Hills Flyers band there was a Brass Captain and two Lieutenants, a Woodwind Captain and two Lieutenants, one Drum Line Captain and one (or more) of his four Lieutenants, a Dance Line Captain, a Color Guard Captain, and a Majorette Captain as well as the Drum Majors. They had to line up a few people deep to make room for all the bands on the field.

The announcers first went through the smaller bands and their results. When it came to the 5A division, the Forrest Hills band stood at attention. It was their way of showing respect for the other schools in the division.

The Forrest Hills band received all Superior ratings. So did South Washington. Before announcing the overall top band, the judges first awarded the caption trophies. Trophies were given in every category: Brass, Woodwinds, Auxiliaries, Percussion and Best Overall or Sweepstakes finish. It seemed like forever until the High Percussion honors were given. The announcer was speaking and everyone on the Line was quiet, "For 3rd place Percussion honors, with a score of 97.51 Swiss County High School!"

All of the Swiss County drummers went crazy.

The announcer continued, "Folks, I want to let you know that the difference between first and second place this year is incredibly close."

Lucy rolled her eyes, if you were on either South's or Forrest Hills's Lines, this was nothing new. The announcer made the same speech every year. In fact, in the past five years the combined differences between the two lines probably didn't add up to ONE point.

"With a score of 94.76.... the South Washington High School percussion ensemble receives second place honors."

Lucy and the rest of the Line started jumping up and down, but her eyes were drawn to the field. She watched as Sam went out to receive the award. It must have been tough for him to walk out there knowing that Jerm and the rest of the Forrest Hills line were about to receive the first place trophy.

"With a score of 94.9 ... the Forrest Hills High School percussion ensemble receives this year's High Percussion ensemble. Captain, please step forward to receive your trophy."

Jerm cockily strutted out and got the trophy, lifting it high over his head. The rest of the Forrest Hills band was excited. Lucy looked at her band friends—they worked so hard; it would be great if everyone could get a first place award too.

"Now, we come to the overall band awards. In third place, Meadowvale High School."

A section of the crowd went crazy. The South and Forrest Hills marching band members all held a collective breath.

"In second place … Forrest Hills High School!"

The Forrest Hills Flyers were happy, but not nearly as happy as they would've been had they been able to bring home the very large Sweepstakes place trophy.

"And finally, your new Hill County Marching Band Classic Champions … South Washington High School!"

The crowd erupted in cheers and the South band rushed the field. Lucy remembered her freshman year when it had been *her* band doing the same thing. Thus tonight's walk back to the buses was a little defeated. The final scores were close, but South had edged out Forrest Hills. Second place at such a big competition was great, but it also made everyone re-think the evening. The questions were on everyone's mind. *What could I have done differently? Was I the one who lost it for us?* The Line didn't want to rub it in everyone's faces that they had individually won. To the percussionists, their win was as good or better than winning the overall band award. The real bragging rights were in the High Percussion Ensemble trophy that Jerm was carrying.

After a "Great job, we'll get em' next week" speech from Mr. Izzo, the marching band prepared for the long drive home. The Captains knew they had a lot to work on before they saw South Washington the following weekend. There was always some room for improvement and next weekend, they certainly wanted to be the ones to return home with a first place trophy and the Sweepstakes prize.

As subdued as the Line was in front of the band, as soon as they got on the bus the entire section went crazy. Everyone was on a high from the win. The trophy got passed around the bus and everyone took turns using their keys or whatever was handy to scratch their initials in it.

Jerm asked Nevada, "Did you see the look on Sam's face?"

Lucy couldn't help but defend her "other" boyfriend and found herself blurting out, "I actually think he looked like he respected the judge's decision. It's not like he flicked you off or anything."

Nevada and Jerm gave Lucy a weird look. Jerm asked Lucy, "You know this is the guy that called you a bitch, right?"

Lucy looked out the window, "*Allegedly* called me a bitch. It could have been someone else." She tried to keep her voice light.

Jerm rolled his eyes, "Well, anyway, I'm glad we kicked South's ass."

Lucy couldn't help herself, "Really Jerm, it was like some tenths of a point that we beat them by, it's not exactly 'kicking their ass.'"

Adam, who had been listening butt in, "Just who's Line on you on anyway?"

Lucy sighed, "Ours, of course. I'm just saying there's no reason to gloat. You guys saw them out there tonight. If anything, we're going to have to work that much harder to beat them at the Indoor competitions."

Lucy didn't mean to, but she had brought down the excitement level of the bus considerably. She decided it was probably better if she just kept her mouth shut. She leaned back in her seat and thought about what had happened. She was elated that her Line had won, but wondered how it would be seeing Sam tomorrow. She didn't want to gloat, because if the situation was reversed, as it easily could be, she would want him to go easy on her. Nevada nudged her, "What's up, Ms. Quiet?"

Lucy smiled, "Nothing. I was just thinking about how great it was out there on the field tonight."

Nevada nodded, "You know, Homecoming is only two weeks away. Next week a competition, but the week after that, we'll get to have a good time away from the field."

Lucy said, "You won't even recognize me. My dress is awesome."

Earlier that summer Lucy had stumbled across what she had dubbed the Rene Russo dress. It looked very similar to the dress Rene had worn in the Thomas Crown Affair, except it was shorter. Lucy knew she was going to turn some heads with it. She was in great shape from all the marching, had an overall toned look courtesy of her big bass drum, and was tanned from all of the after school practices.

Nevada sized her up in a very seductive way and then promptly ruined the moment by asking, "So, are you going to South's Homecoming too?"

Lucy answered almost honestly, "Yes, actually I am."

With the Captain of South's Line ...

Nevada grumpily turned away and crossed his arms, "I wish you would just make up your mind already."

In the past week or two, Nevada had become increasingly unhappy with the fact that she was dating someone else. He was constantly pressuring Lucy to exclusively date him and not the mystery man from South.

Lucy spoke her mind, "I wish you wouldn't pressure me. If you wanted to date someone else you could. We're not exclusive."

Nevada was a guy, and he had, like most drummers, a lot of pride, "Maybe I will."

This was not the way Lucy wanted things to go. She was so happy with the arrangement she had. If she saw Nevada with another girl, she might not be able to handle it. However, Lucy was a drummer too, and just as proud, so she replied, "Maybe you should."

They didn't say anything to each other the entire drive home.

You can hardly blame him …

I know

And if this is how he is now, then how do you think he's going to react if he finds out just who you're dating from South?

He's not going to.

You're playing with fire and you're going to get burned

Consider this a risk. Get over it.

After putting her bass drum away, Lucy looked for Nevada, but there was no sign of him. Maybe it was a sign that this whole crazy ride was about to end. Lucy tried to remind herself of the fun weeks leading up to now, but it wouldn't stop how much it hurt that Nevada hadn't come to say good night.

The following afternoon Lucy was still in a foul mood. She had imagined going to the Homecomings with the great guys she was dating and having a kick ass time at both. As she drove over to his house, Lucy hoped that Sam wasn't in a bad mood. Sam met her at the door and led her downstairs to his basement.

Lucy said neutrally, "I couldn't believe how close our scores were."

"Yeah."

"I wonder what our tapes will say."

"I don't know."

Lucy wasn't sure where to go next. Obviously, Sam was in a bad mood.

"Lucy, it was really tough seeing you yesterday with Nevada."

Lucy let out a sigh of relief; she thought it was the competition that was bringing him down, "Yeah?"

Sam continued, "I thought I could handle you dating someone else, but now I'm not sure if I can."

Lucy didn't say anything. She had been dreading this day, but she knew it wasn't fair to either of them. Being exclusive was kind of an all or nothing thing.

Sam took Lucy's hands and said, "So, I know I'm not the easier decision, but I think you and I really have something. I don't want to just see you one day a week. I want to be your full time boyfriend. Even if we can't ride on the bus together or hang out at school, I don't want you doing those things with anyone else but me. I don't want to give you a time limit to make your decision, but you've had over a month of dating both of us to figure it out. So, hopefully soon you will, because I don't want to have to make the decision easy for you."

Lucy nodded, and said quietly, "I'll have to think about it. Listen Sam, I have to go home and catch up on all the studying I didn't do yesterday."

Sam nodded. Lucy got up to leave. She was halfway up the stairs, when Sam crossed the room and swept Lucy into a passionate kiss. He kissed her soundly for a few minutes before letting her go, saying huskily, "I hope that helps you make your decision."

11

MIND MADE UP

Shako n. A tall, cylindrical cap, usually peaked, sometimes tapered at the top. It is usually adorned with some kind of ornamental plate or badge on the front, metallic or otherwise, and often has a feather, plume, or pompon attached at the top and worn by members of the marching band. Most Battery members tend to hold the chinstraps in their mouths for a more intimidating look. Those in the Pit are not required to wear one.

Lucy stumbled out to her car, breathless from Sam's kisses.

A girl should get a warning before a kiss like that!

The boy can kiss, but I don't think it's entirely fair to base who you chose on who can kiss the best.

So, new solution, how about I drop out of school and transferring to somewhere where no one knows me?

Wah, wah! Listen to yourself, you have your choice of two hot boys and you're getting all melodramatic about it.

Lucy got home and pulled out her diary.

Dear Diary,

AHHHHHH! Looking back through the entries in this thing I remember myself from last year and how all I wanted in the whole world was a boyfriend. I wished and wished and look where it got me. I really only just wanted one. Just one boyfriend to take me to Homecoming and bring me flowers and all that crap. Just one boyfriend to hold my hand and call me at night and tell me I was beautiful. What did I get? Two!! I know, poor me, but now it's time to make the decision and I simply don't want to do it. I really just want to keep my life on hold. They are so different, Sam and Nevada. After wanting Nevada for so long, I won't lie that I thought it was going to be different dating him. It's not that he's still the super hottie that he always was, it's just that there's more of a connection with Sam. But how can that be? I only get to see him for a few precious hours a week. He's always sending me cute messages and when we are together it's just indescribable. Why can't I like Nevada more?!?!? I liked him for SO LONG. What's wrong with me? Everyone tells me how cute we look together, but honestly, I don't know ...

The worst part is I can't even bring any help in. I am desperate for another opinion but don't trust the girls not to tell someone. Who would they tell me to choose? Nevada? Sam? They don't know Sam like I do. If they think Nevada and I are happy, I just wish they could see me and Sam together.

Lucy looked at the page and put her pen down. She wanted so badly to make the easy decision. But her heart was leaning in another direction altogether. Sam had liked her as herself (or mostly herself) from the first time he met her. Something had clicked that day in the theater. She continued writing.

With Nevada, I've been right in front of him for two years. What changed to make him like me? Or was it just the fact that he was just between girlfriends at the beginning of the season? Was he really the player I always thought he was? What makes me different that he won't just love and leave me? And if I do choose Sam, how will the fallout of breaking up with Nevada affect me and the rest of the Line?

Lucy knew it was really none of their business, but since the Line was just a big strange incestuous family anyway, they would all have an opinion. Lucy cringed to think what they would all think if they all knew she was dating the opposing line's Captain. The reputation and friendships she had worked so hard on would definitely be put in jeopardy.

Sam is obviously ready to put a lot on the line (pun intended) by dating me. He would have to deal with the fall out from his own Line as well. Doesn't that prove anything? I guess we'll see how this week plays out.

Melodramatically yours,

Lucy

A pensive Lucy walked into Percussion class on Monday. The good mood from Saturday was still on. Everyone was pumped about the win over South. During the first part of class the drummers sat and listened to the judges tapes from the competition. They were mostly good comments with some specific spots for each section to work on. Overall, Jerm was very happy with the Line's performance. He got up and addressed the group, "Now listen, guys, we have to keep it up, because South is going to be there again this weekend and it's going to be just as close. Now, during sectionals I need everyone to really concentrate on their part of the show. Do what you can to be more uniform and sound like one drum. Add cool visuals, do whatever it takes to make your part better. I'll see everyone after school."

Lucy walked to her next class. She was hurt, but not surprised when Nevada didn't join her.

After school, sectionals were a great distraction for Lucy. Being on the bass line was different than any of the other sections. It was not about sounding like one drum, but really listening and finding your distinct place in the five notes. The boys on the bass line were a great diversion from the confusion that was currently her life. Too soon, sectionals were over and the Line was putting their instruments away. Lucy looked for a moment to get Nevada's attention. He kept busy with his cymbal players and somehow managed to get out of the percussion room without Lucy seeing him leave. She found herself running out to catch Nevada at his car.

Why are you running after him?

I have to tell him …

Tell him what?

There was a moment of sudden clarity with the whole situation.

She shouted, "Nevada!"

He turned around, "Yes?"

Lucy, out of breath, caught up to him and panted, "Well, um, I've made a decision about the whole exclusive thing."

That statement definitely got his attention, "And?"

Lucy gulped and the words just started pouring out, "Well, the thing is—"

Nevada had delivered this line enough times to know what was coming; his heart sank, but he toughed up, "Listen. I get it. Apparently this guy at South is worth throwing away all that we did and had—" Nevada's voice did a very uncharacteristic crack but he pulled it together to say goodbye, "So, anyway, I hope he's worth it. Bye, Lucy."

Nevada got in his car, slamming the door.

Lucy didn't make a move to stop him. She had tears streaming down her face. She didn't know how she pictured things going, but it was nothing like this. She wanted to remain friends with Nevada and obviously that wasn't going to be in the cards for a while. She watched the car drive away and said sadly, "I guess that means you're not going to be my date to Homecoming."

This fact was somehow more depressing than anything else. Lucy had so desperately wanted to simply go with a boy that liked her and dress up and have a good time, but that was before everything got super complicated. She slowly walked over to her car. Tom was parked next to her and loading his quints into his mini-van. He had been taking them home as much as possible to practice for the upcoming individual competitions at Indoor. Tom knew Lucy's moods pretty well and noticed right away that she was upset.

"Hey Luce—what's wrong?"

"Oh Tom," was all Lucy managed to get out before she broke down in tears. She sat down on the curb. Tom had a sister of his own and knew that this one might take awhile. Tom sat down next to Lucy and put his arm around her, rubbing her back as she cried. A good ten minutes later, her sniffles came to an end.

Tom smiled, "That's my girl. Now Lucy, what in the heck is wrong? All I could get out of your incoherent sobbing was something about Nevada and Sam? You weren't making a lot of sense."

Lucy sighed, "Promise you'll keep this to yourself?"

"You got it."

Lucy took a deep breath, blew her nose, and said, "Here's the thing. Before school started, I met this great guy and it turns out this great guy just so happens to be the Captain of South's Line. At the same time, Nevada decides that he likes me and so I date the two guys the same time. Both want me to date them exclusively. So I picked one."

Tom sat a moment, not saying anything. Lucy was worried. It wasn't like Tom to be quiet for this long.

"Well, Luce, when this all gets out, Jerm is going to kill you. And if you didn't tell Nevada who exactly you were with … well, I just hope he never finds out."

Lucy threw up her hands, "I know, I know! I hated hurting Nevada and can you imagine how hurt he would've been I told him, 'Oh Nevada, by the way, you're great and all, but I like the South Captain better than you?'"

"You can't pick who you like, but you should've just been honest from the beginning." Tom said.

"I know that now," said Lucy quietly.

Tom was quiet for a minute and then he started laughing hysterically.

Lucy was outraged, "What are you laughing at?! I've been crying my heart out over here, Tom!"

"I was just thinking that only you, Lucy, could get herself into this kind of mess."

"Thanks Tom, you're a real buddy," Lucy thought a moment, "So, you really don't care that I'm dating our rival Line's Captain?"

Tom considered the facts, "Well, I know you've wanted to date someone for a long time. But I guess I'd have to see you two together to make sure he was good enough for you. However, if it was worth breaking up with Nevada over and possibly crossing the Line over, he must be a pretty cool dude."

Lucy leaned into Tom, "You don't know how much that means to me."

She and Tom got up. Tom walked over to his car, but looked back at his friend, "So, we're all good here?"

Lucy smiled, "Yes. Thanks for always being there for me."

Tom returned the smile and got in his car.

Lucy got in her car and called Sam. He answered on the first ring, "What's up? We just got done with practice."

"Wow, you're really working everyone late. We got done a half hour ago."

"Yeah, well there's this tough Line with a really hot girl drummer on it and we have to beat them this weekend."

Lucy grinned, "I'll bet. Listen, do you think we could meet up tonight?"

"Sure. Since I bet you're as hot and smelly as I am, want to have dinner at WaHo?"

"Yup, I'll meet you there in a few."

"No primping or changing—I want to see what Forrest Hills looks like after a practice."

"I promise, you'll get me just as I am. I'm too tired to make an effort."

"See you there."

Lucy called her parents to let them know she wouldn't be home for dinner. Her emotions were pretty much shot when she pulled up to Waffle House. They had been run all over the place in the past day. She arrived before Sam and got a table in the back. Just when she thought maybe Sam wasn't going to show, he walked up. Green eyes glanced up to see Sam's familiar tall, muscular frame fit perfectly into a wifebeater make his way through the restaurant towards her. At that moment, Lucy knew she made the right decision. Her face lit up and there was nothing she could do to stop it. Her smile was reflected in Sam's face. Lucy got up to hug Sam. After a good strong hug, Sam released Lucy and took a step back to look at her.

"You know, I never get a chance to see how you look at practice," Sam let out a low whistle, "It's no wonder you're the sweetheart of Forrest Hills's drum line."

Lucy was wearing gray cheerleader shorts rolled up and her drum line shirt from last year with Adidas flip flops. Her hair was pulled back into a messy ponytail and tucked behind a visor. Lucy looked down at herself and then back at Sam, asking skeptically, "You sure you haven't been spending too much time in the sun?"

"I just like what I see, that's all," Sam's voice betrayed himself. His tone was serious.

Lucy picked up on it, of course. Just like Nevada, the South senior wanted to know what her decision was. Lucy didn't want to delay her response, "So Sam, you're probably wondering why I called you."

"You missed me so much from yesterday that you just couldn't take it and had to see me?" Sam's voice sounded a little deeper than usual; obviously he thought Lucy had brought him here to break up with him.

"Well, I always miss you, but Sam, I thought a lot about what you said and—"

Sam interrupted her, "I never should've forced you to make a decision. Obviously, I wasn't going to get picked," he continued rambling, "I mean, why would you choose the guy you never see and the Captain of your rival Line?"

Lucy shook her head, "Hmm, that's weird, because even after all those things, I still DID pick you."

Sam's ears must've not been working; his mind was still wondering why he had ever forced Lucy to choose between him and Nevada, so he asked, "Sorry, what did you say?"

"I pick you, Sam," Lucy said shyly.

Sam whooped and all the restaurant patrons turned around to give the back corner booth a strange look. Sam uncharacteristically flushed and asked, "Why me?"

Lucy had a hard time meeting his intense gaze. She fiddled with her cutlery, "You liked me from the beginning and you continued to like me even after I lied to you and even though I'm on your opposing line. I don't know … no guy has ever been like that with me. They always notice my friends first and me later, but with you it was different."

Sam grinned at Lucy from across the booth. They finished dinner and walked out to their cars. Sam pulled Lucy into a tight embrace, "So, I guess I'll see you on Saturday?"

"I'm looking forward to it."

Lucy looked up into Sam's twinkling blue eyes and was momentarily over-whelmed by the warmth and love (!?) that was coming from them.

I made the right choice …

As if to solidify those feelings, Sam leaned down and kissed Lucy softly. From inside the restaurant, someone else saw this last embrace. If Lucy had wanted the following weeks of her life to be easy, she should have simply left the restaurant without the goodnight kiss. Lucy drove home, oblivious to the fact that word was spreading quickly that Lucy Karate had been spotted embracing none other than Sam from South in the Waffle House parking lot.

12

I AM WOMAN!

Rudiment n. One of a set of basic patterns used in drumming. These patterns form the basic building blocks or "vocabulary" of drumming, and can be combined in a more-or-less infinite variety of ways to create drumming music. Some examples include: paradiddle, flam, single roll and pataflafla.

The following day, Lucy walked up to the percussion lunch table. She sat down, taking off her iPod headphones as she did. As she started getting out her lunch, the freshman around her scattered to another table, leaving Lucy by herself.

That was weird …

She started eating her PB and J and looked down at the end of the table where the seniors sat. She tried to catch someone's attention, but wasn't able to.

It's almost like they're ignoring me on purpose.

I expected some fallout from the whole Nevada breakup thing, but this is a little extreme.

Lucy saw Molly frantically motioning at her from the soda machine.

What the hell is going on?

Lucy had a sinking feeling in the bottom of her stomach as she walked to meet her friend. They walked silently to the girl's restroom. The bass drummer didn't bother with chit chat, "What the hell is going on?"

Molly looked down at her black and white Vans and said, "Someone saw you last night."

"So?"

"Lucy, someone saw you and Sam in a very compromising situation."

Lucy's world abruptly turned upside down.

Molly continued, "When were you going to tell me?"

Lucy said quietly, "I thought you would hate me."

"It would've been better to hear it from you than to find out this way. I thought we were friends."

"We are! I just, it got complicated and this is exactly what I didn't want to have happen. I'm sorry."

Molly crossed her arms, "Well, I guess everyone knows. Word got out quick."

Lucy managed to croak, "What is this? Middle school?"

"You and I both know that guys are just as bad as girls when it comes to this stuff."

"How is Jerm taking it?"

Molly shrugged, "He's pretty quiet. And are you sure you shouldn't be asking how Nevada's doing?"

Lucy let out a deep sigh.

Molly asked quietly, "Lucy, are you sure you did the right thing?"

Lucy looked up, tears threatening to spill over, "That's the worst part. I really did do the right thing. Sam's just ... well, I wish they could know Sam like I know him. He's really not a bad guy at all!"

Molly rolled her eyes, "Lucy, hello? Nevada is their boy, and now he looks like a total idiot. Not only have you dumped him, but you've also 'chosen' Sam over him. They *have* to stick up for him. I'm sure they're going to make it really tough on you. I thought you should at least get an advance warning."

Lucy was trying her best not to cry, and managed to say, "Molly, thanks for being a friend and telling me what's up, even though I haven't been completely honest with you. I know I deserve some of this, but it's really just an issue between me and Nevada, not me and the rest of the Line. Who I want to date should be my business!"

Molly shrugged and walked back to the lunchroom. Lucy darted into the closest stall and broke down. All the emotion from the past week had caught up with her and it was too much. Also, she wasn't about to cry in front of the guys.

That's exactly what they would expect me to do. I'm not about to give them the satisfaction.

As her mind jumped around, she wasn't sure how to handle the next hour. Lucy thought about things and decided it was too soon to face everything.

If there was only some way to clear things up with Nevada ...

When the bell rang a few minutes later, Lucy collected herself; she was a part of this Line and had to face the music sooner or later. No matter how much she wanted to skip class and never return, she had worked hard for her spot on the bass line and wasn't about to give the guys any excuse to ... well, she wasn't sure what exactly they would do, but she didn't want to give them any more ammunition than they already had.

Wiping the last of her tears away, Lucy took a deep breath and walked into the band room. She expected the silent treatment and that's exactly what she was getting. The bass line gave her somewhat sympathetic looks, as did Tom, but the seniors were stone faced and Lucy didn't even risk a look at Nevada. She got out her bass drum, stand, and mallets and lined up with the rest of the basses. Lucy looked straight ahead. She was the definition of a committed drummer.

Jerm warmed everyone up. At the end of the warm up, he looked like he wanted to say something before they started running through the show, but thought better of it. It was the longest fifty minutes of Lucy's life, but she thought she had dodged a bullet when the clock showed five minutes left of class. Everyone was putting their instruments away when Lucy felt a tap on her shoulder. It was Jerm.

"Lucy? A word with you before band practice today?"

Lucy nodded; she didn't trust her voice.

Wanting to avoid any questioning, Lucy made it to her next class in record speed and considered her options before her imminent doom in an hour.

This is so NOT the time to sit on the fence.

What can I do?

Tell him the truth.

Lucy ducked into the crowded hall and went to Nevada's classroom. Her former crush was already in class, sitting at his desk, drumming at his seat. Lucy watched as a lock of his red hair fell in his face.

Come on now, you've made your decision and it was the right one. You did not come here to re-crush on Nevada; you came here to straighten things out.

Lucy had no other choice but to go into the classroom. She stopped at Nevada's desk. Fortunately, Nevada's German teacher, Frau Miller, was not the most observant person and didn't notice the extra person in her classroom. Lucy knew she only had a few minutes before the last bell rang.

"Nevada—I need to talk to you."

The cymbal player ignored her.

"Seriously Nevada, I want … well, I want to give you an explanation. I owe you that."

Not even acknowledging her presence, Nevada looked in his backpack and got out his notebook.

"Fine, be that way. But if you want the truth, meet me in the percussion room during this period. I'll be waiting," Lucy was embarrassed that her voice started quavering.

Backpedaling out of the classroom with as much pride as she could muster, she walked quietly and quickly through the halls to the band room and ducked inside the percussion room. Lucy was almost positive this was going to earn her a detention from her Media Studies class, but she didn't care. Pacing around the percussion room she realized this was the stupidest thing she had ever done. Nevada wasn't going to show up and Jerm was probably going to make up some rule to get her kicked off the Line in about an hour. Lucy sat down and put her head between her knees. She wanted to crawl into her bass case, close the lid and never come out. She sat like that for a while until she was aware that someone was coughing to get her attention. Lucy looked up. It was Nevada. He didn't look very happy. They stood staring at each other for a moment. Finally, Lucy patted the ground next to her. Nevada slowly sat down.

"Nevada—I ..."

"I what, Lucy?! What could you possibly say that's going to do you any good right now?"

Lucy's green eyes held Nevada's hazel ones a moment before she said, "Nevada, I deserve everything that you are saying to me. I should've told you exactly who I was dating, even if it meant you would break up with me. For that, you have every right to be mad at me. What I don't deserve, is whatever it is that Jerm is going to pull this afternoon. What I did to you and what happens between us is just that, *our* business. It's no business of anyone else on this Line, in this band, or at this school!"

Nevada was silent for a moment, "Why couldn't you just tell me the truth?"

Lucy had to look away from Nevada's intense eye contact. She half mumbled, "Because I knew you'd break things off with me, and I didn't want that happening."

Nevada was quiet again, "Well, you're right on that."

Lucy, at the risk of sounding clichéd, still found herself saying, "Nevada, you have to believe me when I say that I didn't want things to turn out this way. It just kept going and going and I had convinced myself that it was good enough you knew I was dating someone else."

Nevada rolled his eyes, "Lucy, spare me. I get that you wanted to keep dating me then, but what about now? Why didn't you pick me? Why some loser drummer from our rival Line?"

Lucy chose to ignore the insult against Sam. She told Nevada honestly, "It wasn't an easy decision, but I guess it was because Sam liked me from the beginning. I know you can't probably understand that; you've always had girls like you. It's different for someone like me. No one has ever liked *me* first and in the end, that's why I chose Sam."

Nevada smiled bitterly, "I guess I was too blind to see what was in front of me the whole time."

Lucy wasn't exactly sure how to respond to that other than *DUH!!!*, so she said calmly, "So, any chance you could talk to Jerm and try and talk him out of whatever it is he's going to try and pull?"

Nevada considered his options; none of which he really liked, "No. I will not talk to Jerm out of respect for his position, but here's what I will do. I agree that this is really just something between you and me." He chewed on his lip a moment, "I will not show up this afternoon. That way it will just be you and Jerm and you can tell him exactly what you told me."

Lucy gulped, "Fine, and Nevada?"

He looked at her hopefully, "Yes?"

Lucy half-smiled, "I really am sorry."

Nevada stood up and left. Lucy sat in the percussion room until the final bell rang. She was in the middle of collecting her thoughts when Jerm walked in. He was, of course, not alone. The rest of the seniors (minus Nevada) collected around him. Out of curiosity, some of the juniors and underclassmen showed up as well. Lucy shrugged, obviously, there wasn't going to be a lot of privacy on this. Lucy stood up slowly.

"What's up, Jerm?" Lucy asked in her most cheerful voice.

"I think you know."

"No, I don't know."

"It's about your boyfriend."

"What about my boyfriend?"

"Your boyfriend? The one you dumped Nevada for, just happens to be the Captain of our opposing drum line? Or did that fact just happen to escape your attention?"

"No, Jerm, it did not escape my attention. What I want to know is which member of *this* Line saw me and Sam last night and decided to spread it around like we were all a bunch of girls?"

No one spoke up.

Crossing her arms, Lucy continued, "Because last time I checked, it's not a crime to kiss your boyfriend good night."

Jerm ignored her comment, asking, "Has anyone seen Nevada around? He was supposed to be here."

Lucy smiled sweetly, "Actually Jerm, I saw Nevada last period. We had a private conversation and decided that what happens between us is our business and not yours."

"That may be true, but back to your boyfriend—"

"He has a name, Jerm. You know his name is Sam."

"Fine, what I want to know is how are we supposed to know that you're going to be loyal to this Line? You lied to Nevada, so how are we to trust that you're not going to run off to Sam and tell him everything about our show? For all we know, you've copied our Indoor music and the entire South Line has access to it."

Green eyes flashing dangerously, Lucy said icily, "First of all, my relationship with Sam is not your concern. Second of all, how dare you question my loyalty to this Line?! Turn the situation around, Jerm. Would you give one of the guys this much crap if they were dating a majorette from South?!"

Jerm didn't say anything.

"Well, would you? Probably not. So I don't want to hear for one more second about whose Line I have loyalty towards. I am on *this* drum line. I play second bass and who I date has no effect on that whatsoever."

"Fine, but as your Captain I still have the right to suspend you from playing this week's game."

"On what grounds?" Lucy was shocked.

"Disrespecting your Captain."

Lucy was stunned. She never dreamed Jerm would actually stop her from playing. She said quietly, "Are you sure you want to do this, Jerm? You know Friday's game is our last practice before the competition."

"Well, if our score suffers, maybe you should have thought about that before you started yelling at me."

"I was not yelling!" yelled an infuriated Lucy.

"I'm sticking by my decision. You're suspended from Friday night games until I decide just how loyal you really are."

"But Jerm …"

This punishment was a really low blow for Lucy. Nothing made her happier than performing during half time or goofing around in the stands. Tears were threatening to spill over and Lucy willed them back. She was NOT going to break down in front of everyone.

"What? Do you have anything else you'd like to share?"

"No," Lucy said, her lower lip trembling.

"Fine. You will dress for the game and march down with the Pit, but if you should so much as pick up your carrier, you can forget Indoor."

Lucy quickly walked off and got ready for band practice. She whipped on her Oakley's so no one could see the tears escaping her eyes.

13

AFTERSHOCK

Carrier n. These metal devices allow stationary drums to be strapped to a moving i.e. marching percussionist. New technology has allowed tenor and snare drummers carriers to be worn under the uniform, allowing for a more seamless look. Bass drummers carriers are worn over the uniform.

Lucy struggled to get through band practice that Tuesday afternoon. She played her part the best she could, but her heart wasn't in the notes or drill.

What's the use of playing if I don't get to play on Friday?

Shake it off. Sam is worth it.

Is he? It would be so much easier with Nevada …

Easier, maybe. The right thing? Not so much.

That's another thing, how do I tell Sam what happened? I'm pretty sure this is not going improve relations between him and Jerm and that's the last thing I need right now.

Lance had gathered the rest of the basses during one of the water breaks, "Guys, this whole thing with Lucy—"

Mark interrupted, "It's unbelievable!"

Nathan and Jared nodded their heads.

Mark continued, much as he and Lucy fought, he didn't like seeing her get pushed around, "Well, I think a show of solidarity is in order."

Nathan caught on, "That's right. We're the bass line and if one of us doesn't play, none of us plays."

Lance was considering his options.

Jared spoke up, "You know she'd do the same for us."

And it was true. Lucy loved each of the guys in her section and they all knew it. Well, ok, sometimes she wanted to kill Mark, but that's just how things were. When it came down to it, she was an integral part of the basses.

Lance finally gave his opinion, "Alright guys. Let's see a show of hands. Who wants to sit out the game on Friday night with Lucy?"

Everyone immediately raised their hands.

"Well, I guess that decides it. Now, we have to keep this to ourselves. I don't want anyone breathing a word of this to ANYONE else on the Line ... especially Lucy. Who she wants to date is her business, but we're going to have to make her sweat a little bit longer."

Lucy looked across the field and saw the bass line sitting around talking.

They're probably talking about me ...

Wow, I really would've thought out of everyone, these guys might actually be able to see my side of things.

Guess I was wrong.

A new batch of tears slipped out. Seeing her section gossiping about her was like salt on an open wound.

Someone getting suspended from a game was news that traveled fast throughout the band, as was the rumor that The Girl on The Battery was dating South's Drum Line Captain. Lucy tried her best to stay out of the way, but she could feel everyone's stares on her throughout practice. Just like with Nevada and Molly, she knew that Mandy and Gina were going to be hurt that Lucy hadn't kept them in the loop. She knew she was going to have to do some explaining and wasn't looking forward to it.

Lucy wasn't the only one lost in her thoughts that afternoon. The drum line had a terrible practice. Everyone was completely distracted by what had happened between Lucy and Jerm. The section that was usually always at attention, always on beat, and always correct on drill, was uncharacteristically out of step.

Lucy booked it out of the band room after practice. She typed into her phone to Sam.

>> *Swings. Now.*

The reply was almost instant. >> *C U in 10.*

Lucy was glumly sitting on a swing when Sam walked up.

"Now is that any way to greet your boyfriend?"

"Sam! Everyone on the Line knows about us."

"Oh?"

"Yeah, someone saw us last night and now the whole Line … correction, now the *entire* band knows."

"Oh."

"Yeah, and Jerm suspended me from Friday night games until he gets his head out of his ass."

Sam chuckled, "Wow. I didn't think he'd take things this far."

Lucy swung a few moments before asking, "If you don't mind me asking, what exactly happened between the two of you?"

Sam looked at her skeptically, "Lucy, my dear, I know you know the answer to this. What is *always* the cause of guys acting like this?"

It took Lucy a minute, "A girl?!"

"Bingo! He's probably still carrying a grudge from the summer between our sophomore and junior years. We were both away at this musical camp. Can you believe he was my roommate?"

Lucy practically fell out of the swing, "No way!"

Sam grinned nostalgically, as if remembering some crazy prank, and continued, "Believe it or not, we actually became pretty good friends."

"You? And Jerm? Were friends?" Lucy had trouble wrapping her head around this fact.

"Sure were."

"Wow. You would never know it."

"Well, long story short, I ended up dating this girl who he originally liked. I think he would claim that I 'stole' her away and by 'steal' I mean that she liked me better and he couldn't handle it. Plus, he said some completely crazy things about me."

Lucy asked incredulously, "*That's* what this whole macho competitive thing is based on?!" She added quietly, "Wow, this girl must've been quite a catch."

Sam put his finger under Lucy's cheek, "She's got nothing on you."

Lucy blushed. Somehow, her no good very horrible bad day was turning out way better than she thought it would. They swung for a few moments in silence, before Lucy asked, "So, you think he's just abusing his power? Since he can't go after you, he's going after the next best thing?"

"I think so. Really Lucy, I think your only option is to just keep on the best you can. Be the best bass drummer you can be."

"Yeah," Lucy was still a little glum no one was on her side.

"And don't worry, I bet there will be some surprises at the game on Friday."

"What are you talking about?"

"Let's just say, I've heard you talk about your section and something tells me, they are not going to take Jerm's decision lightly."

"I hope you're right," Lucy still wasn't completely cheered up, but was beginning to brighten, "You know, at least now that everyone knows I'm dating you, there's no reason to hide it. It will be great to have you as my date for Homecoming. No more sneaking around!"

"That's what I'm saying."

"Thanks for meeting me out here. I really needed to see you."

Now it was Sam's turn to blush, "Well, little lady, that's no problem at all. Anything for my girlfriend."

Lucy spent most of the night on damage control. She had a three-way conversation with Gina and Mandy and was doing her best to explain to them what had been going on over the past month. They weren't pleased with her for keeping them in the dark, but excited at all the controversy it was producing. Lucy had to bite her tongue to keep from spilling insults about Jerm to Mandy.

"I guess I've never seen Sam close up. Is he really cuter than Nevada?" asked Mandy.

"Yes ... I mean, maybe not in the conventional sense, but to me ..."

"What are you going to do if Nevada starts dating someone else?" Gina wanted to know.

"Ughhh, I don't even want to think about that, but I guess he has every right."

"How bummed are you that you can't march on Friday?" asked Mandy.

Lucy couldn't hold it in any longer, "I'm pretty freakin' bummed. And I'm also completely pissed at your boyfriend. Talk about mad with power."

Mandy remained silent. Lucy knew she should apologize, but she didn't want to. She really was pissed at Jerm, so she continued, "Listen Mandy, I'm not going to make you choose sides or anything, but I'm just mad because Jerm is taking out a personal grudge on me and that's not cool."

"Well, maybe you shouldn't have talked back to him. He is your Captain. Don't you think he deserves some respect?"

"I would give him respect if he had handled this whole situation with more professionalism. He shouldn't have announced to the whole Line that he wanted to see me after school! It was like broadcasting to everyone, 'Come after school and watch Lucy get torn apart!'"

Gina broke in, "Hey girls, this isn't going to go anywhere. I think we should all just agree to disagree."

"And whose side are you on?" Lucy and Mandy asked at the same time.

"Well Lucy, I just don't know why you didn't tell us about this from the beginning."

Lucy rolled her eyes, "I see how it is! Listen, just once I wanted something for me! And you know how things get around between boyfriends and girlfriends; I was worried that Jerm would find out."

Mandy said bitterly, "Thanks for trusting me."

Lucy muttered, "Well, it's happened in the past."

The junior bass drummer was not surprised when she heard a click. Lucy continued, "I really am sorry, Gina. I should've trusted both of you. It just got out of hand."

"I guess," said Gina in a frosty tone.

Lucy attempted her most bubbly tone, "I would love for you to meet Sam. Maybe this weekend?"

"We'll be at the competition …"

"He'll be there too."

"Oh, right. Let me think about it, Luce."

Lucy walked through the rest of the week like she was on autopilot. Her grades improved because she had nothing else to concentrate on. Her parents were unpleasantly surprised when she received detention for skipping class. Lucy wasn't ready to apologize to Mandy yet and no one on the Line except Tom would come within a ten-foot radius of her. Lucy suspected they were waiting to see what the results of the competition would be this weekend. Furthermore, she was used to the attentions of Nevada at school and was constantly reminded how much the redheaded cymbal player was around and just how absent Sam was.

Cut him some slack—he goes to a different school.

I know. I'm just wondering if I rushed my decision.

What do you honestly feel when you see Nevada?

Lucy looked ahead as Nevada walked to class. She squinted her eyes and saw that he was talking to Christina, an underclassman on the Dance Line.

At the moment, honestly, all I really want to do is yell at that girl to stay away from my boyfriend.

He's allowed to move on. You did.

Don't remind me. I just thought our relationship would take a little longer to get over.

At that moment, Nevada's hazel eyes looked back and locked on Lucy's green ones. She looked away, embarrassed at the hurt in her eyes.

All too soon it was Friday night. Lucy debated skipping the game, but knew if she did, there would be no chance at her playing at the competition the next day. Grudgingly, she got together her uniform and beret and headed to the game. She had to watch as one of the freshmen marched *her* bass down to the field and played the National Anthem on the field. Lucy had a lot of low moments in her life, but this was worst. The first quarter drug by and with five minutes left in the second quarter, the band made its way down to the field to warm up. Lucy numbly sat and watched. She looked down at the Line and noticed that they looked like they were missing someone … *wait a minute.* Lucy slowly turned around and saw the rest of the basses waving at her from the top of the stands. A slow smile slid across Lucy's face. She ran up and in a very uncharacteristic moment, there was a bass line group hug. Lucy looked incredulously at her section, before stopping on Mark, "Even you, Mark?"

"Especially me, Luce."

Lucy found herself getting choked up, "You guys are the greatest section a girl could ever ask for, but you do realize that Jerm is going to kill you?"

"We're willing to take that chance," said Lance.

And sure enough, Jerm had realized that he was missing a section from his Line. He wasn't the only one. Members of the band looked up and saw five bass drummers sitting in the stands.

Mr. Izzo walked up to Jerm and asked in a tight voice, "Jerm, you do realize we're competing tomorrow?"

"Yes, sir."

"And the purpose of marching without the basses is?"

"Um … well, see …" Jerm knew once he started explaining things that Mr. Izzo would insist the basses ALL march, so he came up with the best response possible, "I was reading this article and sometimes it helps when a section is missing so the rest of the Line can really focus on where their part fits in."

"What about the other sections? Don't you think they need to hear the bass line?"

"Um, yes?"

Unfortunately, it was too late. The rest of the marching band was lined up and ready to march out on the field.

"I don't want to see this happen again, Jerm. We already have six snares and one less is a lot different than missing the entire bass line."

"Yes, sir."

Lucy and the basses laughed as they saw Jerm awkwardly run over to get into his spot on time. The missing section knew there would probably be hell to pay, but watching Jerm get in trouble and then his positively ungraceful run made it worth it. For Lucy it was extra special knowing that she really did have some-one—four someones—on her side.

14

FRIDAY NIGHT LIGHTS

Rimshot n. The sound produced by hitting the rim and the head of a drum at once, with a drum stick. Rimshots are usually played to produce a more accented note, and are typically played loudly. There are two standard types of rim shots in marching percussion. The first, more common shot is called a "ping shot". In a ping shot, a drum stick hits the head and the rim at the same time, with the bead very close to the rim. This produces a high pitched sound. The other, called a "gock," is produced by putting the bead of the drum stick close to the center, the rim making contact closer to the hand than in a ping.

Overall, the halftime show ran smoothly. Lucy and the bass line moved to the middle of the stands so they could get a better view. They cheered a little too enthusiastically after the drum solo, gathering strange looks from the other people in the stands. As they sat listening, there were some definite holes where their part would've fit in. After the band marched off the field, the bass line had a few things to discuss.

Lucy sighed, "You know what happens if we lose tomorrow?"

Lance nodded, "The rest of the Line is going to totally blame us."

Nathan said, "Not necessarily. I think everyone agrees that Jerm went a little overboard. Maybe they can justify what we did."

Jared rolled his eyes, "This is so not what we need going into Indoor."

Lucy shrugged her shoulders, "I just wish I knew what I could do to make Jerm less of a prick about this whole thing."

Mark watched as the Line was making its way back into the stands, "I think you can start by avoiding him as much as possible."

Lucy smiled, "Definitely already on my 'to do' list. And guys?"

They all looked at Lucy.

"The rest of the Line may hate us, but when it comes time during Indoor, I know we're going to hear our names called when Best Bass Line is announced."

Everyone shared a smile.

To say the stands were uncomfortable that evening was a massive understatement. It was hard to march the show and not notice that an entire section was missing from it. Rumors were flying through the marching band. Lucy smiled as she heard what was going around.

"... It's all Lucy's fault. I know she forced the guys not to march. Only she would pull something like that ..." *As if!*

"... I heard this was all South's way of sabotaging our line. I bet Sam doesn't even like Lucy ..." *He does so!*

"... I heard Lucy and Jerm actually started fighting ... and Lucy won!" Lucy laughed out loud when she heard that one.

"Does that mean Nevada's single?" *That's **so** not what I wanted to hear ...*

Halfway through the fourth quarter, Jerm motioned for Lance to meet him on the track below the stands. Jerm crossed his arms, "What in the hell was that all about? You think you can just show up on the field whenever you feel like it?!"

Lance looked down at Jerm. With more bravado than he actually felt, the sophomore responded, "Well Jerm, you run your section one way, I run mine another."

Jerm turned bright red, "Let's not forget who is running the entire section!"

Lance smiled dangerously, "And we all see how well that's turning out."

Jerm took a deep breath, "What do you want me to do? The rest of the Line is pissed that one of the sections punked out the night before a competition. If we lose tomorrow to South, it's going to be all your fault."

"Well, maybe you should've thought of the consequences before benching Lucy. You think we're our best as a section when one-fifth of the group is missing?"

"Maybe Lucy should've thought about the consequences of dating Sam."

Lucy, who had been trying not to butt in, leaned over the fence, yelling down at her Captain, "Jerm, I thought we discussed this earlier—who I date is my business!"

Jerm looked up, and tried to ignore the band members that were leaning in and listening intently, "Lucy, I don't remember asking you to be a part of this conversation!"

Lucy took a deep breath. She needed to save face in front of the Line, so she went for the low blow, "Jerm, why don't you tell everyone what this is really about?"

"I don't know, Lucy. You tell me. How about your complete inability to listen to authority? Your lack of decency to the guys you're dating? Your unbelievably horrible taste in a boyfriend?"

Not missing a beat, Lucy shot right back, "No, I was actually thinking of the summer when you and Sam were friends."

Now everyone in the band was at attention and listening in on the Drum Line's conversation. Fortunately, Mr. Izzo was across the field talking with the other school's band director, which left only the band parents to gawk and wonder at what was going on. Overall, the band was relatively well behaved and disciplined. There were occasional scuffles between some of the sections and the usual pranks, but nothing like this had ever happened.

Jerm looked up at Lucy. She stared back at him, green eyes locking with steel blue, not backing down. If he wanted everyone to know what happened that summer, she was more than prepared to fill them in.

"Lucy, I think you should head back to the band room."

During the confrontation between Lucy and Jerm, Lance had been exchanging looks with the bass line. They had all agreed at practice that they were in this thing all the way. Lance wanted to send the message that if you messed with one of the bass drummers; you messed with all of them.

Lance barked out, "Bass line, ten hut!"

Lucy and Jerm turned and stared at Lance as if he had lost his mind, but the remaining bass line members responded by hitting their drums in unison.

Lance continued calling out orders as he walked up to the stands, "Bass line, get your drums on and get in formation."

Jerm and the rest of the band could only watch as Lucy scrambled up the stairs and joined the bass line, putting her drum on and walking up out of the stands to where the drum line traditionally gathered before marching back to the school. Lance clicked and the basses started playing the bass cadence, Self-Proclaimed Huguenots, marching all the way back to the percussion room, leaving a dumbstruck Jerm in their wake. Back in the school, everyone took off their drums silently, unsure what to do or say. Then Lucy started laughing hysterically. She couldn't help it; this whole situation was surreal. It only took a few seconds before the rest of the basses joined in. It was a good five minutes before they finally caught their breath.

Lucy wiped tears from her eyes, "Seriously guys, you go ahead, I'm going to try and see if I can't work things out with Jerm. And Lance?"

Lance looked up.

"That was a seriously brilliant move."

A new round of giggles started up. The guys high-fived each other and left the room. Lucy changed out of her uniform and went out to wait at Jerm's car. She had a feeling that he wouldn't want to see Mandy tonight. While Lucy was waiting she called Sam to fill him in about what had happened.

Sam said, "You tell Lance that if he ever wants to switch Lines, we could use someone with *cajones* like that."

Lucy laughed, "I will. I'll try and introduce you two tomorrow. See you then?"

"I'll be the one in the South drum line jacket."

Lucy hung up the phone laughing. She heard someone walking up behind her. Taking a deep breath, Lucy turned around, surprised to find Jerm behind her, with an equally odd look on his face. Lucy hadn't been expecting Jerm so soon and Jerm had been lost in his own thoughts walking out to the parking lot. Jerm, she had to admit, cleaned up nicely in his traditional post-game "uniform:" well worn dark blue jeans, a fitted white t-shirt and one of his crazy belt buckles.

"Come on Lucy, let's take a walk."

Lucy looked at Jerm strangely, but nodded. They began walking through the parking lot down to the stadium. It was a nice night; the team had won, Summer had finally given way to Fall and there was a cool briskness in the evening air. Given the range of events in the past week, Lucy was glad for the quiet time—with each step the anger and resentment she was feeling towards Jerm seemed to dissipate. She couldn't tell, but she thought Jerm might be calming down as well. They walked all the way down to the field, which was still brightly lit. It was a stark contrast to earlier in the evening. The awkward pair stood overlooking the field. Finally Jerm broke the silence.

"I don't know what I'm going to do with you, Lucy."

Lucy thought a moment before answering, "She must have been really special."

Jerm looked over at Lucy, "I—this isn't about—shit—yeah, she really was and I thought he was my friend."

"Do you think I don't know what that feels like?"

Jerm was unresponsive.

"Look at who you're dating right now, Jerm. Mandy. Did you even once, for a second, consider dating me?"

Jerm gave the female percussionist a weird look.

Lucy rolled her eyes, "It was a hypothetical question, Jerm, but put yourself in my shoes. I have two beautiful friends and for the better part of our friendship have had to watch as they constantly dated the guys that I liked. But I didn't hold it against them. Well, I tried not to hold it against them; sometimes it was really difficult. Eventually, I would try and come to terms with the fact that they were a better couple than he and I ever would've been. So, I know exactly where you've been, but I got past it a long time ago."

"Yeah, I dig."

"So then, maybe you can let go of this grudge against Sam … and me?"

"Maybe, but I can't let the bass line go unpunished."

"I know, but that was their decision, not mine."

Jerm was thinking.

Lucy asked, "Would you expect anything less of the snares?"

Jerm looked up, "Well, after your section's last stunt, I think we're going to have a chance to test that theory."

"Mr. Izzo benched you?!" Lucy had to bite her lip from laughing.

"Yes, he did," Jerm pouted.

Lucy tried to comfort her Captain, "Doesn't matter. Think of it this way, next week is Homecoming, and that doesn't really count as a game anyway."

Lucy was trying to think of a solution that would make everyone happy. She couldn't take back the things she had done or said, but the Line would have to work together if they were going to have a shot at Indoor or the competition tomorrow. She asked, "I can't go above Lance's position, but what if we offer to clean all the drums?"

"Including polishing the cymbals?"

"Especially polishing the cymbals—it's the least I can do for Nevada."

"Fair enough."

"Just be sure to talk it over with Lance. Hopefully the two of you can kiss and make up."

"OK."

"Can we head back now? I'm sure you're going to have some explaining to do at Waffle House."

"Yeah."

They started walking back to the now deserted parking lot.

"Hey Jerm?"

"Yes?"

"I think Sam is ready to talk whenever you're ready."

Jerm didn't say anything, but Lucy didn't expect him to. There was only so far you could push a teenage boy in an evening. Jerm turned to Lucy when they had reached his car and looked like he wanted to say something, but extended his hand instead. Awkwardly, Lucy shook it.

"Night Lucy."

Lucy walked back to her car shaking her head.
That was weird ...

15

ANY GIVEN SATURDAY

Captain n. The overall leader of a main section in the marching band. Larger bands will generally award this position to more experienced individuals and may have a person in this position for the following sections, Brass, Woodwinds, Drum Line, Guard, etc. Responsibilities most likely include discipline, leadership, and running sectionals. The only person higher in rank to a Captain is the Drum Major.

Arriving home, Lucy was far too wired to think about sleeping. After saying hello to Pam and changing into her comfies, she quickly signed online. It had been entirely too long since she had talked to Cartwright213. Lucy chewed on a pen as she waited to see if he was on. She missed their easy talk and banter, as well as his much needed insight into her love life! Lucy was bummed when she didn't see his name pop up in her buddy list. She dawdled around and was about to sign off and to get some much-needed sleep when *Cartwright213* popped up. Lucy instantly began typing.

bassgirl17: Howdy stranger!
Cartwright213: (yawn)
bassgirl17: Where have you been, young man? Isn't it past your bedtime?
Cartwright213: Can't a guy have a life?
bassgirl17: Fine, fine. Listen, do you have a minute? I could really use some advice.
Cartwright213: Umm, yeah, go ahead.

Lucy looked at the screen, noting that something was off in her online buddy's voice. Lucy looked at the clock on her computer … it was after 1AM, maybe that was the reason. Realizing that she had to be up in a few hours to head out to the competition, Lucy decided to let it go.

bassgirl17: Well, never mind. It can wait. I know it's late.

***Cartwright213**: K.*

Lucy signed off quickly, more than a little hurt. On the other side of the computer *Cartwright213* sighed deeply as he saw *bassgirl17* sign off without saying anything else to him, this was not how he wanted things to go. He stared at his computer screen, wishing he'd had the guts to tell her who he really was, but knew that would only further complicate things.

Lucy dragged herself out of bed the next morning, showered quickly, and made one side trip on her way to the school. She cautiously crept into the band room, looking around for a friendly face. There were not a lot to be found. The band had definitely noticed the missing section last night. Although it had been amusing at the game, the seniors realized it could affect the competition today. Lucy tried to offer a smile to some of the upperclassmen, even though internally she was seething.

... *Always looking for someone to blame if your own section is the one that messes up. Of course it's one bass drummer's fault if the entire band gets second place. No pressure, guys.*

Lucy scooted into the percussion room. Jerm was already there and apparently had spread the word that things were cool again on the Line. Lucy smiled to herself; this was the great difference between guys and girls. Lucy could trust that once Jerm had let everyone know that everything was water under the bridge, it would be just that. There would be no lingering, bitchy feelings going on. Lucy also knew that sometimes refined sugar could go a long way towards an apology. The junior dragged her bass drum case out, and placed the four dozen still warm Krispy Kreme donuts on top of it, "Hey guys, come and get it! Drummers need sugar to survive, or hadn't you heard?"

The collected drummers dove into the green and white boxes. Lucy shared a wink over the boxes with Jerm as she grabbed one of the sugary donuts and went in search of Nevada. She caught him coming into the school and tried her best to remain pleasant, "Peace offering?"

Nevada shrugged, "Too soon, Luce."

He continued walking. Molly came around the corner to see Lucy lamely holding a donut and staring at the delicious smelling confection with entirely too much intensity.

"Something wrong, Luce?"

"He didn't want my donut."

Molly didn't have to ask who "he" was. She replied, "You kind of broke his heart. I think I can understand why he doesn't want your donut."

Lucy shrugged, "I did not break his heart. He's Nevada, demi-god of the Drum Line. Breaker of hearts across the Forrest Hills marching band. I don't think I had any real impact on his life."

"I wouldn't be so sure about that."

"Really?"

Molly linked her arm through Lucy's as they began walking back to the band room, "You didn't see yourself the way we did. He was definitely a smitten kitten."

"Really?"

"Yes, and trust me, I don't think you've heard the last from him. He doesn't strike me as the type to go down without a fight."

Riding to the competition on the drum line bus was a very subdued affair. Lucy reverted to her old seatmate and sat with Tom, glad for his comforting presence. Finally arriving at the competition, Lucy watched as the Line quickly dispersed throughout the campus of the high school that was hosting the event. Lucy was moping along when someone came up behind her and whispered in her ear, "Hey there, bass girl."

Lucy tried to ignore, again, the goosebumps that went down her arms. She turned around and looked at Sam. With the exception of their vividly opposing drum line jackets, they made a pretty cute couple. Lucy was wearing low-rise, slightly flared jeans with her drum line shirt and jacket. Sam was wearing well-worn khaki cords, a fitted white t-shirt, and his drum line jacket. This was the first time they had been "in public" together in front of their respective bands and that made Lucy and Sam something of a celebrity couple. The rumors had been flying through both bands.

Lucy thought it would be weird, but more than anything, she found herself very relaxed and was glad she didn't have to hide her boyfriend any longer. Sam bent down and kissed the top of Lucy's head, "A lot can change in a week."

"Amen," Lucy replied.

"Is there anyone you want to avoid?"

Lucy looked around, "You know what? No. I want to be with my boyfriend and I don't care who that pisses off. What about you?"

Sam smiled, "Sounds good to me. I guess the real question is, whose band are we going to sit with?"

Lucy scrunched up her nose, "Not sure. Let's just walk around and see who comes to us."

Sam and Lucy held hands and walked through the various stages of the band competition. There were the smaller bands getting ready, already warming up for their big moment on the field. Auxiliary members were putting on copious amounts of make up and massive amounts of hair spray to complete their looks of uniformity. While they walked, Sam and Lucy passed by members of both bands. They were, of course, pointed and whispered at. Lucy was pleased to see a few jealous looks coming her way—and not just from members of the South band. Lucy looked up at Sam, with his good looks and crazy talent, she was still surprised that he wanted to be with her. She wasn't anything really special.

Just a crazy junior with an affinity for playing a large bass drum. Just like every other girl my age …

Wow, I'm really lucky Sam likes me.

Sam and Lucy finally gave up and decided to sit in the stands. It didn't take long for each of the Lines to find out where they were. Lucy could see Jerm (with Mandy), Nevada and the rest of the seniors at the top of the stands, while Sam noted a lot of his Line had gathered just to the bottom of the stands. The pair found the whole situation rather amusing. Lucy was surprised when Fred approached them. As the Drum Major, he didn't have to care too much about everyone's opinion, but she knew it was a big gesture for him to come sit with her.

Lucy looked at him gratefully and then said, "Sam, I'd like to introduce you to my Drum Major and very good friend, Fred. Fred, this is my boyfriend and South's drum line Captain, Sam."

The guys shook hands.

Fred laughed, "Well, Sam, I'm not going to lie to you. I had to come here and see what everyone was talking about."

Sam smiled and replied confidentially, "I trust you'll make an appropriate report back to the band?"

Fred nodded with mock severity, "Well, you know, she did sit out a game for you. I had to make sure that you were worth it."

Lucy was turning red, "Thanks, Fred. I'm sure I'm perfectly capable of deciding that on my own."

Fred continued talking as if he didn't hear Lucy, "She is my oldest friend, you know. We've been friends since first grade."

Fred looked up and nodded. Lucy and Sam were very surprised when they turned around and saw a girl standing behind them. It was Becca, one of the Drum Majors from South Washington.

"Hey Fred."

"Hey Becca."

Lucy interrupted, "You guys know each other?"

Fred and Becca nodded.

Becca said, "Well, I had to see what all the commotion was about, too. I wanted to meet the girl who stole the heart of South's most eligible bachelor."

Lucy smiled. She liked Becca instantly. As Drum Major, Becca was like an honorary drum line girl. The four chatted until it finally came time to join their respective bands. Lucy couldn't put a finger on it, but she was pretty sure Fred had something of a crush on the pretty drum major from South Washington. She would have to tease him about it later. Lucy had been enjoying this uninterrupted time with Sam so much that she could hardly believe most of the day had passed. Lucy wasn't much into PDA's, but didn't mind that Sam gave her a lengthy kiss goodbye.

"You wouldn't be trying to keep my mind off the competition, would you?"

"Why, whatever do you mean?"

"Kissing a girl like that, she could end up forgetting her name and the drill to the drum solo."

"Well, as I said last week, may the best Line win."

Lucy nodded, "I'm just looking forward to next weekend. It will be a nice break, getting all dressed up and doing normal high school things."

Sam smiled, "I can't wait."

With one final kiss, Sam and Lucy went their separate ways to find their own Lines. Lucy strolled dreamily up to the equipment truck and began unpacking her drum. She was still in a romantic place and didn't join in to all of the usual pre-warm up joking and singing. A certain redhead tried to ignore the content smile on the second bass's face, wishing he could've been the one to put it there.

Lucy's Sam filled thoughts were interrupted when Henry signaled everyone to warm up. He had heard what had happened the night before and wasn't impressed with the complete lack of camaraderie. The details were still a little sketchy, but he hoped his Line would bounce back for this performance. As a whole, the Line was intense and very focused, but lacked their usual energy. Everyone was trying to put the night before out of their heads and concentrate at the task at hand. Like the previous week, Lucy felt that time moved in fast forward and before she knew it, they were marching onto the field, keeping in time to the single beat from Jerm's snare. This week, however, Forrest Hills drew the last spot of the evening and had to wait and listen as South performed. It was almost surreal as they took the field. Lucy now knew what Sam and his Line must have felt like the week before. When it came time for the drum solo, Lucy could feel the eyes of the South drummers mentally picking her Line apart. She knew they had nothing to fear; the drum break was clean and the drill was performed with military precision. Lucy's head snapped up as she realized the break was over and they were already into the Dance Line feature. Suddenly, the entire show was over and they were marching off the field. Lucy knew they had done an excellent job, but somehow couldn't shake the feeling but she didn't think her Line was going to win the competition this evening. They were lacking the spirit they usually did in performance. Technically, she knew they had scored all the notes and licks, but when you compared their section to the rest of the band, there was definitely something missing. She hoped the judges wouldn't pick up on it.

After what seemed like forever, the scores were finally ready. Lucy was glad she was wearing her gloves this evening, or else she would be frantically chewing her nails. The Captains and Lieutenants of the different bands had taken the field. As the announcer made his way through the smaller divisions, Lucy tried to ignore the eyes of some of her fellow band members.

Why can't they just take pride in the show they just did? Why do they have to look for someone to blame if they don't get the beloved first place trophy?

Lucy wasn't alone. It seemed the rest of the bass line was getting unwanted glares as well.

Finally, the caption trophies were being given away. Lucy perked up when the Percussion Ensemble caption was called. She kept hoping to herself that they would win, but was not completely surprised when Forrest Hills was called for second place. The score was very close, as it had been the week before, but this time the Forrest Hills Line was not the victor.

The band looked depressed. They knew it wasn't a good sign if the drum line did not win Best Percussion Ensemble. So when, much to everyone's elated surprise, the overall Best Band award went to Forrest Hills, everyone went crazy! The drummers tried to act happy for their friends, knowing that they had a part of the best band trophy, but it wasn't the same when they lost best Percussion Ensemble to South.

Everyone slowly walked back to the equipment truck. Lucy knew that she was going to get blamed for the second place finish. She wished she could get back on any bus but the drum line bus. Lucy was surprised to see that Tom was still holding his seat for her. She slid in closest to the window and tried to ignore the glares she knew she was getting.

Jerm was the last to board. He let out an ear splitting whistle that got everyone's attention and addressed the entire bus, "Now guys, this past week hasn't been easy for any of us. I know a lot of you want to blame Lucy and the rest of the basses for our second place today, but I want you to blame someone else. Me."

Jerm let his words sink in for a moment. Lucy looked up, surprised at where this speech was going. Jerm continued, "I let a personal grudge affect my ability to Captain this Line. I think Nevada said earlier in the season, that if we win, it should be because we are the best line. Well, you know what? We weren't the best line tonight and the judges saw it. I'm here to say that from this point on the Forrest Hills Drum Line is one unit, one sound and that we're going to seriously kick some ass come Indoor."

Jerm's voice had gotten more and more excited, prompting everyone to applaud this last statement.

"Finally, just to show that everything is cool, I have a question to ask. Lucy, would you and Sam join me and Mandy for dinner before Homecoming next weekend?"

All heads on the bus turned towards Lucy.

Put on the spot, Lucy managed to mumble, "Umm, ok, sounds great."

"Great then. From now on, it's about being the best Line, no questions asked."

16

HOMECOMING (PART I)

Lieutenant n. In a large marching organization, a Lieutenant is in a leadership position but is subordinate to the Captain. This individual helps the general running of a large section of the marching band (Brass, Woodwinds, Guard, Drum Line). In the Drum Line, a Lieutenant might be chosen for each individual section.

Lucy spent the rest of the ride home wondering how the heck she would get out of her double date with Jerm and Mandy. When she had pictured Homecoming over the past week, it was usually just she and Sam and an unbelievably romantic evening. Then again, four months ago, she pictured herself sitting home alone on that particular Saturday evening.

Maybe it won't be as bad as you think ...

Maybe monkeys might fly out of my—

But seriously, Homecoming is going to be as good as you want it to be. So what if it's with Jerm and Mandy? I bet it will still be memorable.

Fine. I promise to have a good attitude. Just me, my boyfriend, my best friend, and the Captain who hates us ... I can't wait!

Just consider it a risk and be quiet.

As she got off the bus, Lucy was surprised to find Mandy walking next to her. She took a deep breath and said to her friend, "Good job tonight, Mandy."

"Thanks, Luce."

"So, I, um, about Homecoming ..."

"It was my idea. I felt bad about how things were and I thought this might be a way of well, an apology ..."

"Really?" Lucy's voice brightened.

"Yeah. After the events of the week, *especially* the game on Friday night, I think I can understand why you wanted to keep Sam hidden from everyone."

Lucy let out a deep sigh and said, "You don't know how much it means to hear you say that."

"Well, no matter what happens, I think we're going to look back and say we did the right thing by making Sam and Jerm finally get over themselves."

"It definitely won't be boring."

Mandy nodded and the pair walked into the band room together.

The week flew by quickly. Everyone seemed to take the loss to South's Line as motivation to redouble their efforts. Afternoons were spent practicing for the Indoor Competition and nights were spent doing homework and preparing for the next week's Midterms. Lucy could barely believe that she was waking up and it was Friday already. She sat a minute in bed and reflected on the week. Her super secret project, with the help of Molly, was going well and would be revealed tonight at the game. Lucy had enlisted her friend's help and it had gone a long way to repairing their differences.

The Homecoming game Friday night was low key. As there was no competition the next day, the band was far more relaxed than the previous Friday. They had their first place trophy and the Homecoming half time show was a hokey little number incorporating this year's theme, "The Way You Look Tonight." Lucy had managed to smuggle her secret project down to the field and was now getting ready to pass it out before the Line marched out on the field. Lucy looked across the track and saw Jerm sitting by himself on the sidelines. She felt bad, knowing that this was his senior year and his games were numbered. It was kind of her fault that he was sitting out, but then again, now he would understand how it had made her feel. Quickly, before they walked out on the field, Lucy placed black armbands on each of the guys left biceps, over their uniforms. The members of the Line were impressed by Lucy's handicraft. "For Jerm," she murmured as she moved onto the next percussionist. The Line was once again all smiles as they marched onto the field.

Jerm looked out over the field as the band began playing the Homecoming song. He cocked his head as he looked at his section, noticing that each member of The Battery was sporting a black armband. Jerm smiled, he had a good idea what it was for, and who was behind the prank. It made sitting out the show a little bit easier.

To say Mr. Izzo was less than happy after the show was an understatement. The Line had quickly taken off the armbands before stepping off the field, but people in the stands had definitely noticed. He approached the drummers in the band room after the game demanding to know where the armbands had come from, "People were approaching me at the game asking if there was a member of the band who had died! Do you know what kind of position that puts me in?! I demand to know who was behind this!!"

Lucy knew the Line was whole again when no one would say whose idea the armbands were or where they had come from. Whatever punishment Mr. Izzo passed down to them would be worth it. Lucy left the percussion room with lots of pats on the back. The struggle between the band director and the drum line was old as time itself.

Saturday morning, Lucy smiled as she woke up and remembered what day it was. She looked over at her dress and shoes, which she had already laid out. Now all she had to do was get through the day! After rubbing her eyes and stretching, she signed online.

Snarejockey1: Morning sleepy head.
bassgirl17: Sorry I didn't call you back last night …
Snarejockey1: No worries. We still on for 6 tonight, right?
bassgirl17: Can't wait!
Snarejockey1: Two weekends before the real fun starts!
*bassgirl17: I know. So, you're **positive** it's cool we go with Jerm?*
Snarejockey1: I'm sure. I promise I'll be on my best behavior. Did you talk your mom into a later curfew?
bassgirl17: Yes, I managed to get another hour out of her.
Snarejockey1: Awesome!
bassgirl17: Do you have something specific in mind?
Snarejockey1: Just wait and be surprised. I gotta go teach some lessons, I'll see you later tonight.
bassgirl17: p's

Lucy sat back, looking forward to her upcoming day. She was about to sign off when a familiar name popped up on her screen.

Cartwright213: Getting ready for the big night?
bassgirl17: Not yet. How long do you think it takes for me to get ready anyways?!
Cartwright213: Hey, I'm not implying anything. I just know how girls can be.

Lucy leaned back from the computer and smiled, obviously Cartwright was no longer in the funk he had been in the week before.

bassgirl17: Well, what about you? Did you find a date?
Cartwright213: Yes, actually, I did.
bassgirl17: Well, that's good news.
Cartwright213: Sort of.
bassgirl17: What do you mean, sort of?
Cartwright213: We have to go with her friend and her friend's lame-o date.
bassgirl17: Why is he "lame-o?"
Cartwright213: It's complicated and too long a story for today.

Lucy thought of her own situation and wondered for the briefest second if the person on the other side of the computer was Jerm. She shook her head—impossible.

bassgirl17: I can dig it—maybe you can tell me about it later.
Cartwright213: We'll see. Have fun tonight!

Lucy signed off and went to go try and study until it was time to get ready.

At exactly five o'clock, Lucy hopped into the shower. For once, Lucy took her time, actually blow drying her hair and curling it. Then she dug out some make up she had managed to scrape together and carefully put it on. Finishing up with her signature scent, Clinique Happy, Lucy looked in the mirror, happy with her reflection. She smiled to herself, and continued smiling when she saw a familiar PT Cruiser pull up in her driveway. Lucy's parents and Sam exchanged pleasantries while Lucy gathered up her purse, pashmina, and flip-flops to change into after the dance. Sam's eyes almost popped out of his head when he got a good look at Lucy. Lucy twirled in a circle so he could get a good look at the short black and white dress complete with strappy black heels. After posing for pictures, the pair hopped in Sam's car and sped off to Asanebo. The couples had agreed to meet at the girls' favorite sushi restaurant.

Once in the car, Sam admitted huskily, "Lucy, in case you didn't realize it, and if I haven't told you enough, you are absolutely beautiful."

Lucy, always one with a smart-ass comment, was speechless. Tonight, with her boyfriend next to her, she did feel very beautiful. She looked over at Sam. Sam cleaned up *very* nice. He was wearing a black pinstripe suit, with a white shirt and gray tie. Lucy wondered if his shoulders could look any broader. He finished off the outfit with his two-tone black and white Doc Martens.

"You don't look half bad either," Lucy returned the compliment.

"Well, no one's going to be looking at me anyway. Oh, look in the back seat … I think you'll find something you might like."

Lucy quickly turned around and started digging through practice pads, music, and drumsticks, before finding a clear florists' box. Lucy squealed as she opened it. He remembered! Lucy's favorite flower was the Stargazer Lily. Sam had gotten the florist to create a beautiful corsage; all centered around one large and awesomely fragrant lily. Lucy couldn't wait and slid it on her wrist.

Sam smiled, "Well, I wanted to be the one to put it on for you, but it looks like you've got it under control."

Lucy leaned over and gave Sam a big kiss on the cheek, "Thank you, Sam. It's beautiful."

"Just like my date."

They pulled up to the restaurant. Lucy knew that Mandy and Jerm were already there because her Captain's recognizable 1977 Ford Fairmont (known as The White Car) was already in the parking lot. Lucy took a deep breath, took Sam's arm, and together they walked in. Mandy waved them over. Her friend looked fabulous in a low cut black dress and elegant upswept hair. Jerm, like Sam, could look good when he wanted to.

Dinner went better than Lucy expected. Everyone was acting very civilized and Mandy and Lucy were doing their best to keep conversation going. They had decided before dinner to stay away from all things band related, and stick to safer subjects like politics and religion. When desert arrived, Lucy let out a deep breath she didn't even know she had been holding. As they finished, Lucy looked over at Mandy, who took the hint.

"Well, I need a new coat of lipstick. Lucy, want to come with me?"

"Sure thing."

"You two behave yourselves," Mandy called out as the girls headed for the bathroom.

As Lucy reapplied a coat of Satin Secret, she told Mandy, "Wow, I thought things were going to go so much worse tonight."

"Me too. But, I guess we've both been surprised. And hey, by the way, I am so proud of you!"

"Why's that?"

"Uhh, hello Lucy? Have you gotten a look at your date? He's like, incredibly hot!"

Lucy smiled, "Well, Jerm cleans up nice too."

The girls shared a smile in the mirror. At that moment, they heard a loud crash and dishes breaking. Lucy and Mandy shared a worried look and then ran out. Jerm and Sam were wrestling on the floor. The girls did their best to jump in and break them up. This was easier said then done, given that the dresses they were wearing, beautiful they may be, did not lend themselves to breaking up a scuffle between two teenage boys. Finally, some of the busboys were able to get in between them. Lucy and Mandy, red-faced, surveyed the damage. Their section of the restaurant was in ruins: tables were turned over and soy sauce was everywhere. Jerm was holding his eye.

Mandy looked over at Lucy, "I'll handle this."

Lucy grabbed each of the guys by the arm and hurried them outside. Lucy knew Mandy had access to her Dad's platinum credit card and would make sure this whole situation was taken care of. Lucy was glad. She didn't want to be blackballed from her favorite sushi restaurant.

As soon as they got to the car, Lucy took a deep breath and was about to start yelling when Sam put a finger up to her lips. He started talking instead, "Lucy … I uh, well, I think I may have mashed some wasabi in Jerm's eye. We should probably take him to the ER and see if he's ok."

Jerm, hand still over his eye, nodded angrily.

Lucy couldn't even believe what was happening. This was supposed to be a night of romance and dancing, not trips to the emergency room.

Sam said, "I'll drive."

At that moment Mandy came out. She looked at Lucy, and Lucy just shrugged her shoulders, "Mandy, your boyfriend's eye is full of wasabi, apparently. We have to go to the ER."

A lesser girl may have gotten more upset by the situation, but Mandy was made of tougher stuff. She grabbed Jerm's hand, "Lead on."

17

THE WAY YOU LOOK TONIGHT

Clean vs. dirty adj. A section of the drum line (snares and tenors) is considered "clean" or having a "clean sound" if all players play the notes at the exact same time, causing them to sound like one drum. A bass line will sound clean if you hear a consistent sound with no breaks. A "dirty" Line is one where not all the players are drumming the exact same way or, in the case of a bass line, a lot of stopping and starting and inconsistent patterns.

If I looked up the definition of uncomfortable in the dictionary, I would probably find a picture of this car ride.

It's not so bad.

Just look at us ...

Mandy was in the back trying her best to comfort the obviously pained Jerm. Lucy was tense and angry. She had been waiting so long to have this romantic dream night and now it was definitely on its way to being thoroughly ruined. Sam was trying his best to not only drive but also to staunch the flow of blood that was coming out of the side of his mouth. Lucy and Mandy were trying to exchange emotions through the rear view mirror and not having a lot of luck. After what seemed an eternity, they finally arrived at St. Joseph's Emergency Room.

Sam got out of the car and opened the door for Jerm, who continued to glare at him from his one good eye. The guys had still not uttered one word to each other, or anyone else. The formally attired foursome drew some strange stares as they walked into the ER. They had just signed Jerm in when the Mandy's cell phone started ringing. The two couples had told their friends they would be arriving at the dance around 9PM and when the appointed hour arrived and there was no sign of either couple, people started getting curious. Mandy had also

105

put in a call to Jerm's parents to tell them their beloved only son was currently sitting in the ER. She was very careful not to elaborate on the details. Mandy, Sam, and Lucy had decided that the rest of the parents were on a need to know basis and they definitely did NOT need to know exactly what happened.

Mandy had hung up her phone, when it started ringing again. She mouthed the word "Gina" to Lucy and stepped outside. Lucy was sitting, very uncomfortably, between Sam and Jerm. It was like a surreal dream. The three of them, dressed to the nines, Sam bleeding from his mouth, Jerm still holding a hand over his eye in the middle of an ER triage area. Lucy was going at great lengths not to touch or look at either one of them. The silence was thick enough to beat with a gong mallet.

"So?!" Lucy couldn't hold the question in any longer; the words practically burst out of her.

Sam and Jerm looked away from each other.

Lucy continued, talking to both boys, but her body language was definitely speaking to Sam, "I think the least you could do is tell me what the hell you two were doing back at the restaurant."

After an eternity, Sam spoke up, "Lucy, what happened back there is between me and Jerm. It doesn't involve you."

At that moment a nurse stepped into the triage area and said, "Jeremiah Stanford?"

The Forrest Hills Drum Line Captain got up to follow the nurse, but not before saying pointedly, "Sam, she deserves to hear the truth."

Lucy and Sam watched as Jerm walked back into the ER. They were quiet again. Suddenly, Lucy felt like she didn't really know the guy sitting next to her. Had she missed something? Was this fight some sort of one time occasion? Who was the guy who had been wrestling at the restaurant?

"Sam? Are you going to tell me the truth?"

"I'm not too proud about what happened this evening, Luce."

"So, you're not going to tell me?"

"I have no idea what he's talking about."

Give the man a chance to speak.

No. I'm sick of listening to you. I don't want to hear his explanation. I want to go to the dance!

You sound like a six year old.

"Sure you don't. Be that way," Lucy stood up, and looked directly at the Sam, "I don't have anything to say to you until I have an explanation. I'm going to this dance one way or another. Who knows? Maybe Nevada would like to dance with me …" At this point Lucy felt tears running over and knew she was about to burst. She ran off in the direction of where Mandy had gone. Sam got up and was running after his date when a nurse stepped in his path.

"Young man, we should get a look at that mouth of yours."

"But I—"

"Young man, you really need to follow me."

Sam could only watch desperately as Lucy disappeared outside.

Mandy was outside and finishing up her call with Gina, "Ok, no, I promise, there is no reason to come here. I'll call you soon. Have fun with Jonathan!"

Lucy stood in front of Mandy, tears running down her face. Mandy reached out to hug Lucy. Lucy got it together after a few moments, "I'm sorry, Mandy, I just pictured this night going so differently. I finally meet this great guy and then … well, maybe I should have continued dating Nevada. None of this would have happened if I had just stayed with him."

"Well, Luce that's partly true, but I saw you with Sam tonight and you guys are good together."

"I guess," said Lucy.

"Were you able to get out of them what the fight was about?"

"No, but I didn't really give Sam a chance to explain. I was just so frustrated by how this night turned out."

The girls sat a moment. Lucy looked over at her friend. She had become friends with Mandy and Gina sometime during eighth grade. Lucy had realized that her quest to be "cool" was getting her nowhere and was glad to have been adopted into Mandy and Gina's friendship. Mandy and Lucy had gone on a quest during the summer to find their first jobs and had worked most of their shifts together, flirting and laughing their way through the ugly uniforms and low pay. Lucy took a deep breath, "Do you know why they started hating each other?"

Mandy, no stranger to the opposite sex, nodded, "In not so many words. I mean, Jerm hasn't come out plainly to say it was a 'she,' but that's the only thing that it could be. They're so much alike, they should be best friends, not enemies."

"Your powers of observation will continue to amaze me."

"Thank you, Ms. Karate."

Lucy and Mandy sat in silence before the bass drummer began speaking, "You know what?"

"What's that?"

"I'm going to go ahead and enjoy our Homecoming. I'll completely understand if you'd rather stay here and wait for your boyfriend. But I think I'd have a much better time if you came with me."

Mandy thought a moment, "You know what?"

"What's that?"

"I'll go; but *only* if you promise me that we can crash South's Homecoming next week."

"Sounds like a fair trade. Do you want to go in and try and find Jerm to tell him we're leaving?"

Mandy shook her head, "I just saw Jerm's parents pull up. I'd rather not be there to see Jerm's mom treat my boyfriend like he's a five year old."

"Understandable."

"But what about you? Don't you want to tell Sam where you're going?"

Lucy looked around, "No. Until he's ready to tell me what the hell was going on earlier tonight, I have nothing to say to him."

"You don't know, Lucy, I'm sure there's a decent explanation for all of this."

"There had better be." Lucy tapped her heeled feet on the pavement, "Well, as our only ride over here has abandoned us, I guess all we need now is a Fairy Godmother."

"Lucy? Mandy?"

Lucy and Mandy jumped, turned around and were surprised to see Katie. Katie was a driver for a local transportation company and a regular at the pizza place the past summer. Katie had befriended Mandy and Lucy during some of those long slow afternoons at the restaurant. Katie drove just about everything out there. Mandy and Lucy had seen her pull up in anything from a Lincoln town car to a huge motorcoach. Their friend was tiny, so it was funny to see her behind the wheel of so many huge vehicles. Tonight wasn't that different; Katie was walking over from a Hummer stretch limo.

"Hey Katie, how's it going?"

"Good."

Lucy had to ask, "What are you doing here? Did someone in your limo get hurt?"

Katie rolled her eyes, "High schoolers. No offense gals, but some kids don't know how to handle themselves."

Mandy said laughing, "Well, you can include our dates in that mess."

"Is that so?"

Lucy was also giggling, "Mine is bleeding from the mouth, and hers can only see out of one eye."

Katie looked at the girls like they were crazy.

Lucy wiped her eyes, "Anyway, Katie, how long do you have to stay here?"

"I don't know, at least a few more hours. They booked the limo for a five hour minimum."

Mandy looked at Lucy, who nodded, then said, "Can you give us a lift?"

Katie thought a moment, then smiled, "For my favorite pizza girls, sure thing."

Twenty minutes later, Mandy and Lucy were pulling up to the school. It was kind of difficult to miss their entrance. An eighteen-passenger Hummer limo pulled up, and the two girls popped out. They had already called ahead to warn Gina of their entrance. Gina, social butterfly that she was, had gathered more than a few people to greet them. A lot of the marching band members were there with confused expressions on their faces as two guys did not also get out of the limo. Lucy and Mandy found Jonathan and Gina in the crowd. Jonathan, gallant gentleman that he was, took Mandy on one arm and Gina on the other and escorted them inside. Lucy decided to just blend in with the crowd and let them go ahead. She watched the girls go in and sat down tiredly outside the gym, seeing her evening ending in a bunch of raw fish and a trip to the ER. She wasn't even sure why she had bothered coming to the dance. Lucy looked at the pavement and was embarrassed at the tears that were threatening, again, to spill over.

Maybe this is exactly what I deserve ...

"Hey."

Lucy looked up and was very surprised to see Nevada standing in front of her. He wasn't wearing anything special, but somehow managed to make her heart beat faster in his black leather motorcycle jacket, white t-shirt, and dark jeans. Lucy glanced cautiously around to see if he was alone. He was.

"Can I have a seat?"

Lucy was beyond embarrassed. Not able to trust her voice just yet, she just nodded. Lucy and Nevada sat quietly. Finally, Lucy blurted out, "Why are you here?"

"I needed something to put on my college application."

"Are you kidding?"

Nevada unclipped his nametag and passed it to Lucy.

She read it aloud, "Nevada Petersen: Photography Assistant."

"That would be me."

They sat in awkward silence.

Lucy finally admitted, "So go ahead."

"Go ahead and what?"

"Go ahead and do what you came over here to do."

"And what would that be?"

"I don't know, 'I told you so.' 'Where is your date?' 'Why are you here by yourself?'"

Nevada was quiet a minute. Then he said, "You know Lucy, I heard what happened tonight, and it kind of seems like punishment enough."

Lucy sighed, "You're right. It looked so simple on paper. Buy dress. Go out to eat. Dance and have a good time."

"Well, you definitely got the 'buy dress' part right," Nevada was grinning and looking appreciatively at said dress. The heat in his eyes was definitely pushing all thoughts of Sam out of Lucy's head. He continued, "Plus, I told you a long time ago. I wanted to see what you looked like dressed up. Consider it a matter of curiosity."

She stood up so he could better look at her dressed up self, "Well, now that you've seen me, I guess you're free to go. Mystery solved."

"I guess so," Nevada said and got up.

Lucy ran her pashmina through her hands, "Well, I'm going to try and find a ride home."

"Not before you dance you're not."

"Is that so?"

"Orders from the Photography Assistant himself. That dress is required to see the inside of a high school gym."

Sam isn't going to be happy when he finds out.

Sam should be here then.

"I guess I can't argue with authority, can I?"

18

LAST DANCE

Chops *n. A difficult word to describe, 'chops' generally refers to the ability of a player to maintain excellent musicality even while playing different licks or phrases over a long period of time. Can refer to both wind and percussion players.*

Lucy tried to ignore her intensely guilty feelings as she followed Nevada into the dance. She knew that somehow this would all get back to Sam and no matter what he did; dancing with Nevada wasn't really a good way of patching up things between them.

Still, if he had really wanted to be here tonight, wouldn't he have at least tried to follow me? How about a call? Or a text message?

Speaking of, have you even bothered to check your phone? Maybe he *has* tried to contact you.

Lucy was about to reach into her purse for her phone when she felt Nevada's hand slip around her own.

Oh no he didn't!! You need to stop this! Turn around and walk away from the red-head.

Come on, Nevada is here as my friend and friends can hold hands, right?

Lucy tried to convince herself that she hadn't *technically* done anything that could count as cheating as she allowed Nevada to lead her out onto the dance floor.

Sam was pacing frantically around the hospital. His mouth had been cleaned up (no stitches, one big warning), but while he had been in the ER, he hadn't been allowed to use his cell phone and even worse, the doctors had called his parents. They were waiting for him when he walked out of the ER.

"Samuel Benton Powell!"

With those words, Sam knew there wasn't a chance of him going anywhere near the dance this evening. Mrs. Powell had bellowed loud enough so the entire waiting room could hear. Sam was attempting to move his family outside and thus avoid further major public humiliation when someone began walking toward them. She walked directly up to Sam and got in his face, "You must be the punk who blinded my son!"

To put it mildly, Sam's mom, Beth, didn't take too kindly towards strangers who walked up and started accusing her son of assault. She got between her son and the strange lady, "And just who the hell are you?"

At that moment, Jerm walked out. Like Sam, he still had his suit on; only Jerm's outfit was completed by a black eye patch placed jauntily over his left eye. As soon as both sets of parents saw Jerm, chaos ensued. Beth and Jerm's mom, Julie, started yelling at each other, with their husbands desperately trying to hold them back. Sam and Jerm just stared at each other. Sam could hardly believe that he was the cause of Jerm's new pirate look. Jerm must have caught on to Sam's feelings, "You should feel bad."

"You earned it."

The young men glared at each other, then looked at their parents, silently agreeing on a momentary truce, and snuck outside while their mothers raged on.

"What the hell are you talking about?! What do you mean *I* earned it?! If anything, *you* earned it."

Sam was frustrated with the entire evening, and had no trouble letting anger from two summers ago boil over, "First of all, do I need to remind you that *you* took the first swing? Did you set this whole evening up so you could take a shot at me?"

Jerm replied bitterly, "My *girlfriend* asked me to do this. She thought maybe we could patch things up. I see that you obviously haven't matured in two years. I wonder what Lucy sees in you."

"Keep Lucy out of this," Sam growled, "And what are you talking about 'matured'? Lauren told me what you said about me that summer. If anyone's immature here—it's you."

Jerm looked at Sam quizzically.

Sam scoffed, "You're going to tell me you don't remember calling me a 'prick percussionist who didn't deserve first chair'?"

"Dude, I didn't say that."

There was something in Jerm's voice that made Sam take notice.

Jerm tapped his foot impatiently, "Did she really tell you that?"

"Yes."

"And you believed her?"

"Why wouldn't I?"

"When she dumped me, she told me that you had been making moves on her for a week."

"So not true, dude."

With that, Sam sat down heavily on the curb, "We got played."

Jerm joined his former roommate on the curb, "Yeah we did."

While his eye had been attended to, Jerm considered what had really been behind his punch. Certainly, some of it had come from the unspent anger of two summers ago, but there was another emotion entirely. He realized it would be the same if any of the boys on his Line had been made a fool of. He would've taken a swing for any of them. To Sam, he asked quietly, "What if she was on your Line? What if she had dumped one of your boys? What would you have done?"

Sam took a moment before responding, "I see your point, but don't you think Nevada is capable of taking care of himself?"

"Touché." The former friends were standing in the disaster of Homecoming, when Jerm started laughing hysterically.

Sam asked, "What in the hell are you laughing at?!"

"I have no idea why I'm mentioning this, maybe it's because we're at a hospital, but do you remember Armstrong and the hot dog?"

Sam's memory was instantly jogged and he found himself joining in Jerm's laughter, whooping along side his former roommate. Sam's sides were hurting when he said, "He never saw it coming."

Jerm commented, "So, maybe our girlfriends were right."

"How's that?"

"I overheard them talking. I think tonight was really just a lesson for us to get over ourselves already."

"I just hope Lucy still wants to be my girlfriend."

"What did you do?"

"For some reason I just couldn't bring myself to admit that I was just as much to blame about our fight earlier as you were. She left before I really got to tell her anything."

"Well, man, you still have a chance to change that."

Sam's eyes darted over to his car, which was still parked in the lot, "Will you cover for me?"

Just then both sets of parents came barging out of the hospital.

Jerm nodded, "It's the least I can do."

Sam took off to his car, determined to find Lucy and set the record straight.

Lucy's guilty conscience seemed to drift further and further away as she danced one song after another with Nevada's strong arms around her. This was more like the night she had been dreaming of. She didn't care who saw them or what the consequences would be. Lucy leaned into Nevada and breathed in his spicy aftershave. He usually worked the five o'clock shadow thing pretty well, but it was nice to have him clean-shaven this evening.

Earth to Lucy? If things go too much further, you're going to wreck any future you might have with Sam.

Gazing into Nevada's hazel eyes, Lucy thought, maybe that wouldn't be such a bad thing.

You have to at least hear Sam out. What if this is all a big misunderstanding?

What if it's not?

Just do the right thing.

"Nevada?"

"Yup?"

"I think it's time for me to leave."

Nevada considered her comment, but kept his arms around her waist, "I tell you what."

"What's that?"

"I'll take you home, but not before we get our pictures taken. You look too good in that dress not to have it officially documented."

That's a fair enough request …

"Sounds great."

Lucy followed Nevada to the gym where the cheesy backdrops were set up. Lucy and Nevada joked with the photographer as they had their Homecoming portrait taken.

"You guys sure make a cute couple," said the photographer as he was giving them their paperwork.

"But …" Lucy interjected.

"Now Lucy, it's a nice compliment."

"I'm sure he says it to everyone."

Nevada, who had been around the photographer all evening, *had* heard that particular comment a few times, "But with us, I think he really means it."

A few minutes later, they were in Nevada's old Volvo station wagon and on the way to Lucy's house. Lucy realized the last time they had been in the car, well, it had been an entirely different situation. Nevada also seemed to realize that the circumstances were much different than last time. It was also the first time in the evening they had been completely alone. Nevada, thus far in the evening, had acted like a perfect, if flirtatious, gentleman. However, Lucy sensed that familiar tension was back between them. She had been trying desperately to ignore it all evening, but there were too many emotions conspiring against her. She was after all, just a teenage girl in a dress. All she could do now was hope to hold out until she was out of the car. They sat awkwardly listening to the radio, not saying anything. Lucy couldn't read what Nevada's mood was. She was still feeling guilty, mad, and confused with the way the evening had turned out. They were pulling up to Lucy's driveway when her phone beeped. They both knew who it was. Lucy was desperate to check the message, but knew how unbelievably rude that would be to Nevada.

"Aren't you going to check that?" Nevada was back to his angry post-break up self.

"No," said Lucy quietly and she turned off the phone.

They continued to sit in the car. Nevada was obviously angry, but Lucy wasn't sure exactly the reason. Nevada didn't know what he had been thinking was going to happen tonight, but obviously Sam was still in the picture. The cymbal player had to convince himself that he was just glad to be Lucy's friend for the evening. Too bad that dress was giving him some very "un-friendly" thoughts.

As Nevada waged a war with himself, Lucy decided it was probably best if she just went inside. Maybe something bad had happened to Sam. Maybe something serious had happened to Jerm. She leaned over to kiss Nevada on the cheek, but at the last minute he turned his head and met her lips with a kiss of his own.

Sam drove frantically towards Lucy's house. When he pulled on her street he slowed down, spying a car in her driveway. He squinted his eyes and saw an unrecognizable redheaded male figure and a very recognizable female figure embrace each other. Sam briefly considering confronting the pair, but arrived at the decision that he had already had enough fighting for the evening. He quickly turned his car around and sped off in the other direction.

This doesn't feel right!
For once, I agree with you.
Then stop what you're doing!
Lucy broke the kiss. Nevada's hazel eyes flashed.

Lucy said awkwardly, "I'm sorry. I can't do this. I thought I could, but it's not right."

Nevada pouted, "Fine."

Lucy scooted towards the door, "I'll call you."

As she closed the door, Nevada commented, "You'd better."

Lucy walked in and looked around her room. Was it only hours ago that she was in here getting ready for her big night with Sam? *Sam!* Lucy scrambled to turn on her phone while at the same time turning on her computer. Sure enough, there were a few messages for her—five new voicemails! She listened to them in order:

"Hey Luce—it's Sam, where are you? I got stuck at the hospital. Please call me and I'll tell you everything."

"Lucy, I need to talk to you. I'm really sorry with the way things turned out. Call me back."

"Hey—I'm starting to get worried. Where are you? Call me and let me know you're safe."

Lucy rolled her eyes, if he had really wanted to see her, he would have driven around to try and find her. There were two more messages.

"Lucy, just saw you and Nevada. I guess I can make the decision easy for you. Please don't try and call or see me."

Lucy's heart plummeted into her stomach. She could only barely hear the last message.

"Lucy, it's Jerm. I can tell you the truth of what happened. Call me."

19

(RE)PERCUSSIONS

__Mark Time HUT!__ command. Marking time is marching in one position, necessary when practicing marching commands in a relatively small space as well as keeping the beat while keeping position in a set and is a command called out by the Drum Major. On the first beat after the start marker, lift the left foot. On the second beat, plant it down and start marching in place. This is somewhere between a position and a march. Percussion should not lift their knees nearly as high as other instruments or they'll bash their harnesses; keeping toes on the ground is often sufficient. This can be called while marching or while halted.

"Hello?" a masculine voice asked.

Lucy realized in her shock and disbelief from Sam's last message, she had accidentally called her Captain, "Oh hey, Jerm. It's Lucy."

"Are you ok?" There was real concern in his voice.

"Well, I haven't talked to Sam yet, but I think I really messed up," Lucy's voice was quavering and she knew she was dangerously close to losing control. She vaguely wondered why she was about to spill her guts to Jerm.

"What happened?"

"Nothing happened!" Lucy said quickly and changed the subject, "I mean, what about you? How is your eye?"

"Well, I'll definitely be wearing a patch to the first Indoor competition," Jerm replied seriously.

Lucy tried her best to hold in a laugh, but was doing a terrible job with it.

Jerm obviously heard her, and shouted into the phone, "You think this is funny?"

Lucy had tears coming down her face, "Well, Jerm given this bizarro Homecoming evening I've just experienced, I'm sorry, but I have this picture of you with an eye patch."

"I do have an eye patch!"

Lucy whooped with laughter. When she finally settled down, she asked Jerm, "How did Sam look when he left the hospital?"

"He was pretty bent on seeing you, Lucy."

"Oh."

"Just 'oh'?"

"I think he may have saw something that didn't happen."

"Such as?"

"Nevada drove me home."

"You seriously need help, Lucy."

"Tell me something I don't already know. So, if you do talk to Sam, just let him know I really want to talk to him."

"Why do you think I would be talking to Sam?" Jerm sounded defensive.

"Call it a hunch. Please Jerm?"

"I'll try, but no promises."

"Thanks. Hope your eye gets better."

Lucy hung up the phone and pondered the best way to get Sam back. She was going to have to bring in reinforcements. Her green eyes flicked over to the clock, it was too late to meet up with Mandy and Gina tonight, but first thing tomorrow she would enlist their expertise. Lucy left a message on Sam's voicemail.

"Hey Sam … I don't know what you saw tonight, but you have to know it didn't mean anything. I want to be with *you*. I hope that means something. Please call me."

Feeling motivated the next morning; Lucy woke up early, drove to pick up some bagels and Starbucks (a hot chocolate for herself, ice-blended mocha for Mandy, and a double shot of espresso for Gina), and pulled up to Gina's house.

Lucy knocked on the door, Gina's mom answered, "They're upstairs. I'm not sure if anyone's awake just yet."

Lucy walked in Gina's room and started pulling up windows curtains and turning on lamps. She heard groaning coming from the twin beds in Gina's room.

"Girls! Up an at em'! I have an emergency!"

Mandy was the first one to arise, "Wassamatter?"

"Sam saw Nevada kissing me!"

That got their attention.

Mandy asked more clearly, "What? How? And when?"

"Last night."

"Last night?!" now Gina was wide awake.

"Well, Nevada was at the dance and then he was really nice to me."

Mandy commented, "Yes, I think a few people saw him 'being nice' to you."

Lucy swallowed, she deserved that, "Well, when Nevada drove me home, I intended for nothing to happen. So I went to give him a quick kiss on the cheek and he turned his head and I think Sam was coming over to see me and he saw us and ..."

"Just breathe, girl," said Gina.

Lucy took a few moments, then continued, "So, I got home and checked my voicemail and Sam left one saying for me never to see him or call him again."

Tears overflowed, and Gina and Mandy joined their friend, rubbing her back.

Lucy asked in a watery tone, "So, how do I get him back?"

Gina and Mandy looked at each other seriously.

Mandy patted Lucy's hand, "Don't worry, Luce, we'll come up with something that will get the two of you back together."

Gina commented, "Mandy said you and Sam were super cute last night at dinner. We'll do whatever it takes to get him to listen to reason."

Lucy perked up, "Thanks, girls. I'm pretty sure I wouldn't be in this situation if I had just asked for your help from the beginning.

Mandy said diplomatically, "That's ok, Luce. You're here now, and that's what matters."

Lucy was starting to feel better about the whole situation. Putting on her bravest face she replied, "So, since I sensed we couldn't do this on an empty stomach, I picked up Starbucks and bagels. To the kitchen!"

After coming up with a plan that was foolproof (at least on paper), Lucy decided to spend the rest of the weekend trying to keep her mind off of Sam. Mandy and Gina had stressed the importance of being apologetic, but not clingy or desperate and to give the South snare some space. It was a very difficult balancing act and took actual concentration for Lucy not to drive over to Sam's house and bang on his door and beg for forgiveness. Instead, she studied for the SAT's, took Pam for a walk, and even played soccer with her brother.

To: SWSnare@SWHS.edu
From: bassgirl17@FHHS.edu

Sam,
I looked back through my in-box and was ashamed to see that this is the second apology e-mail I'm sending you in as many months. Like the messages I've been leaving you, I hope you understand that it's definitely not Nevada I want to be with—it's you. I don't care that you go to another school or are the Captain of my opposing Line. All I care is that I get to see your beautiful blue eyes again. Please meet me at your Homecoming? I'll be looking for you.

Your Lucy

Fifth period on Monday was loud. As Lucy walked into the band room, things came suddenly rushing back to her ... the black arm bands from Friday night, the fight at the restaurant, Jerm's eye patch....

Jerm locked his one good eye with Lucy when she walked in.

He hasn't told them ...

Thus far, the true story behind Jerm's eye patch was known only to Sam, Jerm, Gina, Mandy, and Lucy.

It would be so easy for him to just blame Sam and tell them. Have Jerm and Sam come farther in their friendship than they are admitting to?

The guys were having a great time making fun of their one-eyed Captain. When things finally settled down and they were about to begin warm-ups, Jerm walked out and stood in the middle of the Line, "Alright guys, first of all, thanks for your 'support' on Friday night. For those of you who arranged the whole thing, I appreciate your loyalty." He avoided looking at Lucy and continued, "Second of all, yes, I have an eye patch. I will have to wear it through at least the first Indoor competition. No, it doesn't affect my drumming. So, any questions?"

The guys sensed something was missing. Tom spoke up, "We missed you and your new 'best friend' on Saturday night."

"My eye incident happened before the dance. I was in the ER," Jerm said authoritatively, but didn't mention where "his new best friend" had been.

Lucy felt a lot of eyes on her, and was hoping desperately no one would ask the obvious questions. *Lucy, weren't you with Jerm and Mandy before the dance? Where was your date? Why were you late? What were you doing dancing with*

Nevada? Lucy knew she and Mandy had made a big entrance in the Hummer limo, but it was made even more mysterious by the fact that both girls had arrived without their dates. Jerm's being in the ER explained Mandy, but for everyone else, Lucy's missing date was a little sketchy. The female bass drummer looked straight ahead at her drum and did her best to concentrate during class. Her thoughts strayed and class was over before she realized it. She glanced back on her way to her next class and locked eyes with Jerm. She nervously walked up to him.

"Hey Jerm," she said cautiously.

"What's up?"

Lucy stumbled, but managed to convey her heartfelt thanks, "Well, um, I wanted to say thank you for not telling everyone exactly what happened on Saturday night. I just don't think it would have gone over to well."

Jerm looked uncomfortable, "Yeah, well, I would've done it for anyone on the Line. That's what being a Captain is all about."

With that typical Jerm phrasing he turned and walked in the other direction.

20

HOMECOMING (PART II)

*"**Dress Center Dress!**" command. Executed from the position of attention with horns up or down, allow the band members to look down a line to check alignment. If you are in line, you should only see the person next to you; if you can see the line, you are not in it. The move is performed by snapping the head to the left or right with no additional body movement. If the alignment is poor, it should be corrected immediately. The drum line clicks their mallets or drum sticks against the carriers during this call and all band members are released when the Drum Major calls, "Ready front!"*

Lucy went home and tried her best to study for her upcoming Biology exam, but didn't get very far. Her eyes kept glancing over at her laptop, which she was desperate to turn on. The great possibility of her in-box and buddy list was calling her. Lucy was online in a matter of seconds.

bassgirl17: *Thank goodness you're here!*
Cartwright213: *How's it going?*
bassgirl17: *Well, it's definitely been better, that's for sure.*
Cartwright213: *What happened? Isn't Homecoming difficult to mess up? I mean you go to dinner, dance, end of story.*
bassgirl17: *I did all that.*
Cartwright213: *Then what's the problem?*
bassgirl17: *A lot of that was done with, um, someone other than my date.*
Cartwright213: *(digesting that information)*
bassgirl17: *To make matters worse, Sam saw Nevada kissing me and now he won't talk to me. and before you say anything, I DID NOT MEAN TO KISS NEVADA!! He just kind of planted one on me.*
Cartwright213: *Wow.*
bassgirl17: *You ain't kidding. So? What can I do?*
Cartwright213: *Well, the more I hear about this Nevada kid, the less I like him.*

Lucy chewed her lip. That was definitely not the reaction she was expecting.

bassgirl17: Care to enlighten me as to why?
Cartwright213: I'm just letting you know that you are making the right decision to go with Sam.
bassgirl17: Thanks for the encouragement …?
Cartwright213: Nevada seems like this guy who has always had girls fawn all over him and now that one is showing the least bit of disinterest, he's doing anything he can to get her back.
bassgirl17: I don't know about that.
Cartwright213: I would just watch yourself. I mean, I'd hate for him to do something drastic.
bassgirl17: (rolling eyes) C'mon, it's Nevada. He likes me.
Cartwright213: Does he? Or does he just not like the idea of "losing" to some other guy?

Lucy felt like she had been punched in the stomach. She couldn't help but admit that she had felt flattered at the dance when Nevada had been so attentive.
Even more attentive than he was then when we were dating …?
But what if Cartwright's right?
That hurts.

bassgirl17: Ok, I'll watch myself. What about Sam?
Cartwright213: He'll come around. I'm sure of it.

The following week, Lucy avoided Nevada like the plague, which more difficult to do than she originally imagined. He seemed to take her "I can't do this" comment as some sort of weird challenge and Lucy had to get creative in her attempts to avoid him. There had been some close calls, and she was trying her best to remember the good memories she had of her former crush and not the weirdly stalker-esque tendencies that he was currently exhibiting. That same week, Lucy was unbelievably sore and tired. Henry had been drilling everyone constantly. With the first Indoor competition the following weekend, there wasn't much time left to make sure the show was perfect. She felt the worse for her friends who were competing in the individual competitions. In addition to all the practices, they had to make time to work on their own pieces as well. Jerm, Tom, Nevada and the cymbal line were entering the individual competition at both Indoor competitions. By Friday night, Lucy still hadn't heard anything from her supposed boyfriend or whether or not he was going to attend South's Homecoming.

On Saturday afternoon, Lucy was moping around, willing the phone to ring, when she heard it trilling in her bedroom. She scrambled and picked it up, recognizing Mandy's number, "Hey, what's up?"

"Don't sound too excited to hear from me," Mandy joked.

"Sorry, I thought you might be Sam."

"He'll be there tonight, Lucy, just you wait."

"You sure you want to go through with this?"

"Let's consider my options: Jerm is grounded to infinity, Gina is busy with Jonathan, and you are in need of a date for Homecoming."

"I know you've heard it before, but you're the best, Mandy!"

An hour later Lucy and Mandy were ready to go to South Washington's Homecoming. With Mandy's overflowing wardrobe, both girls were wearing different dresses from the week before. Mandy had opted for a red silk Asian style dress with dangerous slits on both sides. Lucy looked stunning in a flowing brown dress that complimented her tan skin. Lucy had also borrowed a red wig from Molly, who occasionally was into the drama scene at school, and completely on board with the "Get Sam Back" campaign. Lucy was worried that even if Sam didn't show that she might be recognized by some of the members of the South's Line and didn't want them wrecking her evening. Looking at herself in the mirror, she didn't think she made a very convincing red head, but Mandy thought it was slightly ironic, "C'mon Luce, imagine what a cute couple you and Nevada would be."

"Ha ha. Very funny. I can't believe we're going to go through with this."

"Lucy, here's what I'm thinking. We're just going to go and see if Sam is there. If he is, we're going to make sure you get a few moments alone with him. If he's there with another girl, I will personally kick his ass. If he's not there at all, we will party like rock stars and come home. No worries."

Lucy looked at herself in the mirror. She wasn't sure she wanted to go through with the plan, "How are we going to get in?"

"Lucy darling, I'm sure they will sell tickets at the door. Besides, if Sam isn't there, who else do we know that goes to South?"

"Ummm. The entire drum line?"

"The last time they saw you, you were Lucy next door. They definitely aren't expecting to see you like this."

"I don't know ..."

"You're officially incognito. So, let's go get in the car and at least enjoy someone's Homecoming. I think we owe it to ourselves after last week's disaster."

Lucy was nervous the entire ride over to the dance. A part of her hoped that Sam wouldn't even be there and that she and Mandy would just go in, dance their hearts out and have a story to tell for years to come. However, there was no turning back as they parked outside of South Washington's gym.

Suddenly, Lucy had a great idea, "I know—let's check the parking lot! If I see his car, we'll go in, if not, we can just go home!"

Mandy shook her head, "Oh no, Ms. Karate. I remember that the deal was, we would crash South's homecoming. One cannot crash South's Homecoming from South's parking lot."

Lucy looked down. Mandy was right. It was time to face the music. The pair began walking towards the South gym. Mandy, not even blinking an eye, bought the tickets and Lucy let out a deep breath as they entered the school. Lucy relaxed long enough to be completely shocked when she turned the corner. There, in the same handsome suit from the week before, was Sam. He hadn't seen her. Lucy grabbed Mandy's hand and sprinted for the nearest girl's bathroom.

"What is it, Lucy? It's tough to run that fast in heels!"

"Sam's here!"

"Is he alone?"

"I didn't see. Will you go check? I could be wrong. What if he is? Do I look all right?" Lucy was babbling.

Mandy looked at her friend. Lucy obviously needed some help with the situation.

"Sure thing, pal. I'll go see if it's him."

Lucy waited while Mandy went back out into the dance. The wait was killing her. Lucy chewed her fingernails.

Why should I be nervous? It's just Sam.

That's your boyfriend out there. Go to him and sort things out. You owe it to him.

What if he still ignores me? I don't think I could take it.

What if you never go and find out?

Lucy had this debate in her mind for quite some time. She was about to go back out to the dance, when Mandy came back into the bathroom. Lucy couldn't read the expression on her friend's face.

"Mandy?"

"Yes?"

"Well?"

"Well, what?"

"Is he out there?"

"Yes."

"And?"

"I'm going home. My work here is done."

"No, no, no Mandy. We talked about me coming to the dance and straightening things out with Sam. We specifically did not talk about Sam driving me home. Remember? I get into trouble when people drive me home."

"I think you should stay."

"Well ..."

"Lucy, you need to hear Sam out. You can't just end things without ever talking again."

"Sure I can."

"Believe me, just go. I'll see you on Monday," Mandy walked out of the bathroom.

Lucy knew she had to face the music. She looked at herself in the mirror, red wig and all and tried to summon all her drum line girl power to go outside. She walked out and it was like time was in slow motion. Sam was there waiting for her. He was alone. Having not seen him in a week, Lucy's heart skipped a beat when she saw his familiar figure. She tried her best to keep her composure, but couldn't help it as a smile broke across her face. An identical smile broke across Sam's face. He held out his hand and led her out onto the dance floor. With perfect timing, the DJ switched from an up tempo song to a slow dance.

"I wasn't sure if you'd show."

"I wasn't sure if you would."

"Touché."

"Sam, I—"

"Lucy, I have to get a few things off my chest before you start talking."

Lucy, never a fan of being told to be quiet, actually nodded silently.

I'm not going to mess this up ...

"I haven't been able to get in touch with you this week because my parents basically put me under house arrest after my fight with Jerm and subsequent unapproved departure from the parking lot. At first I was glad because I didn't want anything to do with you, but then I found myself thinking that you were probably getting the wrong idea."

Which I totally was ...

"But then I was able to convince my mom after laying on the schmaltz pretty thick that I didn't want to miss my senior year Homecoming."

"So you're here by yourself?" asked a very relieved Lucy.

"It would appear that way."

Lucy admitted, "I'm glad."

Sam reached out and gently fingered her wig, "I think I like you better as a brunette."

Lucy's cheeks pinked, "Yeah, well, I wasn't sure who I was going to see from your Line. Anyway, Sam, I—"

Sam asked, "You want to do this here?"

Lucy looked around at all the happy dancing couples. She really didn't want to cause a scene, but she wasn't going to be able to move forward with Sam until she apologized. She took a deep breath, "Yes, I do."

"Ok."

Lucy could feel the arms around her tense up, "What you saw a week ago wasn't anything. It—"

"It sure looked like something."

"I listened to you, will you please listen to me?"

"Yes."

"So, it's like I said in my e-mail and countless phone calls. I don't want to be with Nevada. I want to be with you!"

"You're sure?"

Lucy nodded her head solemnly.

Sam raked a hand through his dark brown hair, "The thing is, I'm not sure I want to be with you. Seeing you and Nevada last week was like a punch in the stomach ... after I had already been punched in the stomach by Jerm. Now, every time I close my eyes I picture you two together and I just can't think that it's not going to happen again. I don't go to your school. I'm not on the bus rides. Hell, I couldn't even be there for the dance last weekend."

Lucy willed the tears pricking the back of her eyes away. She said desperately, "But you're here now. That has to count for something."

"Lucy, you ran the first chance you had and made out with your ex-boyfriend. How do you expect me to ever trust you again?"

The tears that were threatening, now flowed over. Hearing Sam's accusations—

The truth. Those aren't accusations.

Lucy hiccupped, "I'm sorry, Sam. I just, I made a mistake."

"I'll say so."

"So …?"

The couple stopped dancing and Sam removed his arms from Lucy's waist.

"I just don't know, Lucy."

Sam walked away, leaving a devastated Lucy in his wake.

This isn't how things are supposed to go.

How does this end?

He turns around and walks back to me. We get our pictures done and laugh about what idiots we were.

This isn't fiction, Lucy. You cheated on him. People break up for things like that.

But I love him …

Lucy numbly exited the dance. She looked around vacantly at the parking lot and idly wondered how she would get home. She opened her phone, pressing the #2 button, speed dialing the one guy who was always there for her.

21

STORMY WEATHER

Drill n. Although the origin of the word comes from the military definition 'to instruct and exercise in formation marching and movement,' drill in most modern marching bands refers to the actual footwork that makes up a field show and may include a number of different steps and features.

"I really appreciate this, Tom."

"No worries, Luce. What were you doing here anyways?"

"I thought, well, who cares what I thought."

"No dice with Sam?"

"How did you know?"

"You're my best girl, Luce. I think I should be able to understand a few things about you by now."

"Yeah, well I don't think you'd like me too much if you knew what I've been up to."

"I'm sure it's just a misunderstanding. It'll work out, you'll see."

"I thought that, but now I'm seriously doubting every romantic comedy I've ever been sucked into."

"Just give it some time."

"That's all I have, anyways."

"Emergency trip to Krispy Kreme?"

"Nah. I really just want to go home and sleep."

Lucy woke up on Monday morning with two distinct emotions. She was still very much heartbroken over Sam's decision and at the same time completely nervous about the upcoming Indoor competition. In less than a week, she would be on the court as a member of The Battery. Fifth period was totally different now that the competition was so close. Everyone inhaled their lunches so they could get their drums and be ready to practice as soon as the gym cleared. They had marked off the competition lines on the basketball court and spent Fifth period running the drill and music over and over again. During the afternoon marching practices for the band on Tuesday and Thursday, the drum line only had to show up during the last hour of practice.

Finally, on Thursday afternoon, the rest of the marching band was invited to watch the Idiot Indoor Show (as the drummers affectionately named it) that their percussion section had been working so hard on for the past month. As the Line played their last note, they heard shouts and cheering go up from the band. Lucy looked around and shared smiles with her fellow percussionists. *We are pretty amazing …* Between everything that had been going on, the Line had managed to put together an outstanding show.

From the closing set, Jerm walked out in front of the Front Line and addressed the band, "Hey guys, thanks for listening to us today. If you aren't doing anything this weekend, come cheer us on at our first Indoor competition."

Jerm cut an interesting figure these days. No one really knew the exact truth behind his eye patch, but it gave him a weird sexy Captain Jack Sparrow edge that had everyone in the band talking. Lucy thought more than a few people might take him up on his offer to come watch the Line compete. As the Line walked back to the band room, there were lots of pats on the back and good luck wishes from band members. Lucy was on a much needed high as she put her drum in its spot and walked out of the band room.

Sam may hate me, but at least I've done something this Fall that I can be proud of.

During Friday's class, Jerm decided it would be best if they didn't do anything except clean the drums; "We've all worked hard enough, so today and at the game tonight we are just going to be about having a good time."

Lucy thought back to the magical moment when the season started in August—before all the fights and drama. As everyone sat around joking and laughing with their section, Lucy could hardly believe her junior year on the Battery was almost over. After the next two weekends, it depended on the football team to see how long the band would continue to play. Lucy looked outside the band room—not a cloud in the sky! She looked forward to tomorrow. Indoor competitions were definitely one of the most fun things about being on Drum Line.

Performing at the game that night was great. The Line was right on beat and had fun trying to out-do each other with extra visuals. Lucy couldn't stop laughing as the bass line attempted a planets visual, all of them rotating in different orbits around third bass in the middle of trying to do their drill. They barely made it back to their spots on the right count. Not to be outdone, the snare line attempted a stick toss from one end of their line to the other, and failed miserably. Herschel had to finish the show with one drumstick. Lucy was out of breath from laughing as they finished the show and marched off the field.

As they packed their drums away, Jerm told everyone, "I'll see everyone tomorrow morning. We're going to kick some ass!"

Lucy tried to go to sleep that night, but found herself as excited as she was the night before her auditions earlier that Spring. Something else was nagging her. She still wasn't sure how to handle Nevada. Throughout the week, her silent treatment had evolved into *his* silent treatment and now things were just plain awkward.

I've got to set things straight with him.

Tomorrow ...

Lucy literally bounced down to breakfast in the morning. Her mom was waiting for her, good luck banana pancakes ready, "You know Lucy, the forecast is predicting some bad storms later today."

Lucy looked outside and saw nothing but blue skies and Bob Ross happy clouds, "Well, I'm sure it won't affect the competition too much."

"Well, bring your umbrella just in case."

Becky meant well, but Lucy laughed as she imagined herself trying to manage the bass drum, mallets and an umbrella. She went upstairs to pick up her uniform. Henry had suggested, much to everyone's delight, that they drop the formal marching band uniform and dress something closer to the punk feel that Billie Joe and company wore. The guys balked at eyeliner, but were okay with tight black jeans, studded belts, white button up shirts and skinny ties. Jerm and the Lieutenants would be wearing a suit jacket. Lucy and Molly had rejoiced when Henry said it was okay for them to wear skirts. It was so rare that they got to wear something the least bit flattering! The girls had decided on matching plaid skirts, fishnets, a white button up shirt and pigtails. Lucy couldn't wait to see everyone's completed "uniform." They had a brief dress run through on Thursday in front of the band, but running the show today during Prelims would add an entirely different element. Henry had really tapped into something with this show and Lucy couldn't wait to see the crowd's reaction.

Lucy heard a horn beep outside and ran out to Tom's minivan.

"Are you ready?" Lucy asked, referring to the individual tenor competition that Tom was competing in.

"I think so. Just be ready for some surprises."

Lucy smiled, knowing that Tom wouldn't let her, or the rest of the audience, down. He was a born performer.

At the school, everyone moved their own drum into the truck and then got themselves on the bus. The good mood was infectious as they drove towards the competition. Lucy sat with Tom, and tried not to think about who Sam was sitting with or that, in a matter of hours, she was going to see him. Two hours later, the bus pulled up to 22nd Annual Southern Regional Indoor Percussion Competition.

22

INDOOR

Indoor Drum Line n. Consists of the marching percussion and front ensemble (or pit) sections of a marching band. It marries elements of music performance, marching, and theater; thus, the activity is often referred to as percussion theater. Most indoor percussion ensembles are affiliated with high schools. Groups compete on a regulation size court in a gymnasium. Bass drums are "taped" to stop their tones from resonating.

The Forrest Hills Drum Line stepped off the bus into a blustery November afternoon. The sky was clear, but there were some menacing clouds in the distance. The Line had gotten to the competition early so they could support the individual and small groups that were entering the individual competitions. It was the right of any percussionist to try their hand and come up with their own routine and be judged accordingly. Forrest Hills's percussionists were usually well represented. Like most individual competitions at Indoor, the 1st place winners in each category would be asked to perform their piece after the Finals that evening while the judges were tallying the final scores.

After Jerm, Tom, Nevada and the cymbal line had pulled their equipment off the truck and gotten good luck wishes and last minute tips from the rest of the Line, everyone went inside the gym to get a good seat. Each member in the individual competition could choose someone to be their "second." The "second" would wait backstage and help the competitor with their instrument. Lucy was flattered when Tom asked her to assist him. After she helped him unload his quints and helped him secure everything for his warm up, she left her friend alone. Lucy looked around and caught sight of some of the members of the South Line that were also backstage. She glimpsed a recognizable set of broad shoulders. Sam turned around and met Lucy's eyes. She waved at him, but instead of returning her wave, he turned around and ignored her.

Well, he looked at me. At least that's a start.

What are you waiting for? Go over to him.

Sure, because I'm exactly who he wants to see.

Nevada had witnessed the exchange and approached Lucy. He made a typical exasperated guy sound.

Forgetting her silent treatment, Lucy asked, "And what exactly is that supposed to mean?"

"Looks like your boyfriend is ignoring you."

"Well, maybe he's just busy. He's got a solo to prepare for."

Then, and probably because Sam's gaze was intently staring at the pair, Nevada leaned in and whispered into Lucy's ear, "I wouldn't ignore you."

Lucy looked up and saw Sam's eyes darken angrily.

Of course he would see that ... now he's really never going to talk to me.

But then, would you want him to?

What do you mean? Of course I do!

Looks like Sam is letting you go without a fight. At least Nevada is making some attempt.

That is something to consider ...

The cymbal line was first to compete. Nevada had everyone in loose fitting long sleeved black shirts, so they would have maximum movement for their arms. With their gloves on, it was difficult to tell where the player's hands ended and the cymbals began. Watching the windmills and combinations of sounds the different cymbals could make, Lucy was impressed with their routine. Lucy was sure they would win. Year after year, the Forrest Hills cymbal line was the line to "borrow" moves from.

Lucy couldn't keep the smile off her face as she helped Tom set up his equipment on the gym floor. Always unconventional, Tom was wearing jeans and his drum line shirt. Besides the usual whisk and mallets, Lucy was pretty sure she glimpsed some other unconventional ways of getting sound out of the tenors.

Tom started his routine and did not disappoint Lucy's expectations. Between some very difficult playing and visuals he mixed up his routine much more than the average quint player. Tom used all kinds of mallets, a samba whistle, and even the ping pong balls. The crowd went crazy when Tom was finished.

After the other tenors competed it was time for the snares. Jerm walked out, looking smart in his marching uniform. Like Tom, he chose to have a second and Billy helped him set his snare up on a stand. From the moment Jerm's traditionally gripped drumstick hit the drum head to the moment he was finished, the gym was silent. When Jerm saluted the judges, letting them know he was finished, people were on their feet congratulating him.

As Jerm walked off, Sam walked on. Lucy was surprised to see Jerm and Sam actually acknowledge each other. Like Jerm, Sam's routine was technically very difficult and no less amazing. Lucy and the rest of the Line did not envy the judges and the decision they would have to make.

With the Individuals finished, there was nothing more to do than wait to warm up for Prelims. The competition was following the standard procedure. There would be a preliminary meet, and then the Lines with the highest scores would be invited back to Finals in the evening. After everyone got something to eat, it was time to change into their uniforms and begin warm-ups. Seeing the group in uniform was a great way to break the nervousness that everyone seemed to get before a big competition. The Forrest Hills Drum Line had called upon their inner punk and the whole Line looked like some sort of bizzaro Green Day fan club.

Overall, there were twenty-five lines competing at the event. Not all of the lines were as big as Forrest Hills, so there were two separate category divisions at this Indoor competition. There were ten lines competing in Forrest Hills's division. Only four would make it to the Finals that evening. From those four lines, best section trophies and overall best Line would be awarded.

While warming up, Lucy was very nervous. Indoor was a completely different rush than regular marching competitions. At Indoor, the pressure was on in a more intense way. With less people on the court, there was a lot of room for individual scrutiny. Lucy was also terrified about the last minute mallet toss that Lance had decided to add on Thursday. Lucy had practiced the drop a million times, but still felt like she could drop her mallet at any time. Warm-ups were over far too quickly and it was time to walk in and march the show.

They lined up on the court in the opening set and waited for the announcer to ask if the Line was ready to compete. Hearing the opening to "Extraordinary Girl", every other thought went out of Lucy's head. The audience looked confused, but picked up on the show as the Line went into the recognizable chorus. Lucy gulped and it was time for the stick toss. Her mallet connected with her hand for the briefest second and then dropped to the gym floor—right in the middle of a move!! Lucy picked up the mallet as fast as she could and joined her section.

I ruined it for everyone. There's no way we're going to win best Bass Line now.

She got back in step quickly, but her heart sunk as the drop played over and over in her head. Suddenly it was over. The show ended to thunderous applause and everyone marched out. Lucy prepared herself for Lance and Jerm's tirade, but there was none. Lucy looked around. Everyone was crowded around Mark.

Somehow Mark had managed to puncture his bass drum head and had been drumming the last half of the show on a busted drum. No one was sure how this would play out with the judges.

The Line quickly put their equipment away and rushed inside so they wouldn't miss the results. Forrest Hills, as the returning champion, had been the last Line to compete in Prelims. Only the Captains of the respective lines went down to the gym floor to wait with the individual performers from earlier in the day for the results. Lucy took a minute to carefully look at Sam and Nevada on the floor. It was the first time she was able to see them together. There were so many things about them that were the same … both percussionists, both seniors, and both really cute, but the choice was obvious.

Molly commented on her friend's intense stare, "Still coming up with the same decision?"

Lucy nodded, "I really wish I did like Nevada. I mean, he's everything I thought I wanted, but when it comes down to it, the answer is Sam."

Molly nudged Lucy with her Chuck Taylored foot, "He'll come around."

The announcer interrupted their conversation, "Thanks for your patience. We are now pleased to announce the winners of the individual competition from this morning."

Nevada and the cymbal line were awarded the top small ensemble trophy. The announcer then moved to the tenor category, "And in first place … from Forrest Hills, Tom Finnigan!"

The Forrest Hills drummers exploded with ecstatic applause! Tom was grinning from ear to ear as he walked up to accept his trophy.

Finally, the announcer reached the snare drum category, "The snare individual competition was extremely close this year and by a very small margin … Sam Powell, please come accept your first place trophy."

Now it was the South Washington drummers turn to go crazy! Lucy's heart went out to Jerm who looked completely depressed despite having won a respectable second place. She also bore the glares of her own Line as she clapped for Sam, hoping that he would hear her.

The announcer finished by declaring the preliminary scores. Going to the Finals from Division I would be Forrest Hills, South Washington, Cedar Grove, and Warner High Schools. South had edged out Forrest Hills for the overall highest score, so they would be the last to perform.

The Line walked outside in good moods and into a light mist. The sky had darkened considerably while they had been inside. It wasn't raining too hard, but it looked like the sky was going to open up any minute. Sure enough, as soon as everyone had put on their drums, it started pouring. Each of competing Lines had to find a place out of the rain to try and do their best to warm up. By the end of the preparations, Lucy could barely feel her fingers around her bass mallets.

Lance motioned Lucy over, "Hey Luce?"

"Yes, Lance?"

In all the excitement of the Prelim scores and Mark's broken drum head, Lucy had momentarily forgotten her mallet drop. She was instantly re-devastated to have let her section down.

"Listen, about the toss …"

"I know, I'm sure I wrecked it for everyone."

"You did no such thing."

"Really?"

"Yup."

"Are we going to keep it in Finals?"

"Yes, but this time we're all going to carry extra mallets," said Lance. There was something in his voice that made Lucy stop.

"Lance?" Lucy paused, before asking, "You didn't drop a mallet, did you?"

Lance smiled, "Come on Lucy, let's go find some extra mallets."

With a new drumhead on Mark's drum and extra mallets in everyone's pockets, the bass line was ready for Finals. In no time at all, the Line was marching back into the gym. The announcer had introduced them and they were about to begin the show when there was an incredible crash of thunder outside and the lights in the gym went out.

23

LIGHTS OUT!

Matched vs. Traditional grip, technique. The matched grip is performed by gripping the drum sticks with one's index finger and middle finger curling around the bottom of the stick and the thumb on the top. This allows the stick to move freely and bounce after striking a percussion instrument and is commonly used in drum set and tenor playing. To perform a traditional grip, your left hand is turned upside down and the stick rests between the thumb and the hand and on the cuticle of your ring finger. Traditional grip is primarily a technique for snare drummers.

"Who's touching me?"

Lucy recognized the voice as none other than the quick-witted and always humorous Tom. A nervous laughter broke out on the gym floor. The Line still stood in formation on the court and waited for the lights to come back on. They didn't. The gymnasium had no windows so it was pitch black on the court. There was no point of trying move out of the gym, because everyone could hear the storm raging outside. Lucy could hear the crowd talking nervously. There was another huge crash of thunder and Lucy shook. The storm was one of the loudest she had ever heard. Suddenly, there was a whistle. Lucy could recognize Henry's earsplitting whistle anywhere. The gym was silent.

Henry's voice called out, "Alright everyone. The important thing is to stay calm. There's been an issue from the Emergency Broadcast System for a tornado warning in this area. We all need to stay inside for the time being."

The announcer spoke up, "Everyone please remain seated. The competition organizers have gone looking for flashlights."

There was silence, another crash of thunder and then Lucy could hear Jerm's voice, "Hey guys, I don't want anyone running into equipment, so take off your drums, and stay seated with your section."

Without her vision, all of Lucy's other senses were heightened. She took off her drum. There was a weird tension running through the floor of the gym. She could feel the presence of the bass line around her. Lucy blinked to try and see anything, but it was completely dark.

"Luce—how are you doing over there? You're being uncharacteristically quiet."

Lucy recognized Tom's voice to her left. He hadn't moved from the quints opening set. Lucy replied, "Umm … nothing."

"Well, come over here. I want to protect you if the ceiling caves in or something."

"Just a minute."

Lucy, who was not the most balanced person in the room, decided it would be best if she went over to the quints on her hands and feet. As Lucy tried to feel her way through the blindness to where the tenors were, she realized she was in the process of crawling over someone and that she had just put her hand in a most inappropriate spot. Lucy's hand jumped back as if she had touched a flame.

"You sure you don't want to get back together, Luce?" Nevada drawled.

Lucy found herself turning red and was glad that the lights weren't on, she stammered, "No…. I…." she wanted to disappear, "I have to go see the quints."

Sure Lucy, because the quints are going to erase the fact that you just put your hand directly on Nevada's crotch.

"Come by any time."

Lucy could hear the smile in his voice. She finally made it over to the quints when she saw flashlights entering the room.

The announcer's voice spoke again, "Alright folks, looks like it may be awhile until power gets back on in this area. Until the danger passes, we're going to keep everyone in the gym. Also, if you will remain seated, we are going to bring in those percussionists that were outside."

Lucy gulped, since Finals were about to start, about the only place there was room in the gym was the gym floor. Sure enough, within minutes, Lucy could see flashlights leading the South Washington drum line to sit near Forrest Hill's Front Ensemble.

Sam's over there …

And?

In the dark, I could sneak over there and try to—

It's over. Give it up.

As soon as all of the South drummers were seated the announcer spoke again, "I've just had word from the sponsors and judges, I'd like to apologize to all our percussionists, but this competition has been cancelled due to weather."

Boos and hisses came up from the seated percussionists. From the Preliminary scores, South had won, but without Finals, it wasn't a clear win. Finals always brought out the best drumming and the most pressure. What happened in Preliminaries was just that; preliminary. Lucy was completely bummed; she had really wanted to take home the best Bass Line trophy that night.

"It's pretty awesome being first," someone said a little too loudly from near where the South drummers were sitting.

Lucy knew it wasn't Sam talking, but that didn't stop Nevada from commenting, "I wish Sam would just shut up about being first already. It's not like they won Finals."

"I didn't say anything! Quit putting words in my mouth!" came Sam's voice across the gym.

"Quit stealing our cymbal moves."

"Stealing, huh? This coming from the guy who stole my Homecoming date," Sam muttered.

Lucy could feel the shock waves ripple across the floor. This was news to everyone on Sam's side of the court.

"Well, she wouldn't have needed a date if you hadn't mashed wasabi in Jerm's eye!"

All the percussionists on the Forrest Hills side were confused. Jerm had never told them exactly how or why he had started wearing the eye patch. The emotions on the gym floor were definitely escalating. Now that Nevada had basically spelled it out for everyone how Jerm had lost use of his eye and Sam had let everyone know that Lucy had been stolen away from him, the tension between the two lines was almost palpable. Lucy couldn't take much more of the testosterone fest that was going on. It was too much. Lucy had to speak up and she did so loud enough for both lines to hear her, "Alright guys, that's enough! What happened off the court has nothing to do with our Lines and I think we should keep it that way. Can't we just keep this about drumming?"

No one was answering and whatever might have happened next, the drummers would never know. Lucy heard Henry's voice over by the snares, "Alright guys, the storm has calmed down enough so I'm going to try and get us out of here. We're going to go section by section. Just wait until the flashlight comes over and you can safely walk to the truck. Let's go Pit!"

She heard Joe, the instructor for South's Line, inform his Line to do the same thing.

Lucy crawled back over to her bass drum. She knew it would be a few minutes until Henry got to her section. She sat next to her drum and willed that no further comments or insults to carry across the floor. She laid back, propped her legs up on her drum, trying to block out everything, desperately trying to figure a way out of this crazy situation that was her life.

Henry interrupted her thoughts, "Come on basses, let's go."

Lucy picked up her drum and slung it over one shoulder. She followed the flashlight out to the equipment truck and packed up her drum. Outside the gym, there were branches and leaves everywhere. The past hour was like a blur. Lucy knew it meant next week's competition was going to be unbelievably intense. The ride home was uncharacteristically quiet. There was no joking or drumming. With the lights out in some of the towns they drove through, it was almost like being back in the gym. Lucy's brain kept running over the events of the day. Everything had started out so great, only to end with a lot of disappointment.

24

AMERICAN IDIOTS

crab step, technique. There are a number of different ways to move on the field during drill. However, with percussion instruments it often becomes imperative to master the crab step. To perform crab stepping the musician crosses one leg over the other, either marching on the toes or rolling the foot sideways. By marching in this way, percussionists can maintain a smooth playing surface necessary for clean playing.

During fifth period, Monday, everyone got a chair and sat down anxiously, waiting to hear the judges' tapes. They would only be able to listen to the Preliminary tapes, but it would have to do. Somehow, not being able to perform in the Finals had taken the wind out of everyone's sails. It was as if all the hard work and practice had somehow not really been for anything. Tom was especially down—he had really been looking forward to doing his winning tenor routine for the crowd. There were no assurances that he would win again this weekend. Overall, it was going to take a lot to get the Line back up to its former energy.

As Jerm started the tape, Lucy's heart started beating faster. In all the chaos of Saturday, Lucy had forgotten about her dropped stick and was cringing, waiting to hear the judge's comment on the tape. Lucy listened to the routine. She knew exactly the spot she dropped her mallet and a couple of notes.

"What's this? Second bass needs to work on her mallet skills."

In case the judge hadn't been referring to Lucy by the second bass comment, the "her" definitely cemented who he was talking about. Every single member of the Forrest Hills Drum Line looked over at Lucy.

"What? I just dropped my mallet—it could happen to anyone!" Lucy was devastated at letting the Line down.

The judge continued, "—and so does fourth bass."

Everyone's head swung around to glare at Lance. The judge continued rapidly, so there was no time to talk about the dropped mallets. When the judge finished he concluded his comments, "I like your style Forrest Hills, but I'm just not sure you are collectively a Line this year. I hear all the parts, but I don't hear them all together. Your playing is outstanding, great licks, phrasing, and stick work, but I'm not hearing it as an ensemble. Work on this for your next competition and you should be unbeatable."

There was silence after the tape ended. Never had the Line heard anything on a tape like this before. No matter what the differences off the court, they always managed to be friends and make it work on the court. The first reaction was, of course, to be angry with the judge, but something about what he had said rang true. Lucy knew each section was functioning fine, but the Line all together …?

It's like they were missing Johnny Roastbeef. During her freshman year, the Drum Line had weirdly happened upon a Teenage Mutant Ninja Turtle action figure (originally Donatello) while they were practicing early in the season. The turtle had been christened Johnny Roastbeef and went on to be the inside joke of the year. They had even written a cadence about him. In fact, "Do it for Johnny!" was still the rallying cry and good luck chant the Line said before competitions. But this year, the collective energy had been on a series of ups and downs. The events with South's drummers earlier in the season weren't an inside joke. True, it had brought the Line together, but it had done so in a very negative way. Lucy shook her head and snapped back to reality.

"He's right."

Heads whipped around. Lucy smiled; it was Tom who had spoken up.

"We've been practicing and we have all the notes. But where is the heart of the Line?"

No one had an answer to that.

Jerm, who had removed his eye patch over the weekend and was now back to his regular self, barked, "What do you think we should do about it?"

Lucy blurted out, "We need to bond."

The guys all groaned; this was not the answer they wanted.

"How exactly are we going to accomplish that?" asked Jerm.

Lucy had a flash of brilliance, "Well, there's a Green Day concert on Thursday. Maybe we should all go."

There was a murmur of agreement through the sections.

Tom continued, smiling at Lucy, picked up the idea and said, "Think about it—how awesome would it be to hear our show live? Plus, if we all went together …"

Jerm challenged, "What if it's sold out?"

Tom shot back, "Come on, Jerm. We're not talking about front row seats—we're talking about the nosebleed section."

One of the freshman, Morty, spoke up, "My mom works for one of the radio stations. Maybe she can get us a deal."

Tom and Lucy looked at Jerm, challenging him to say anything but "yes."

Jerm sighed and rolled his eyes, "Fine. We'll try and get tickets."

A collective whoop went throughout the room. When it was all said and done, no other section would even dream of doing something like this.

Lucy and Molly walked to their next class together.

"Seriously brilliant suggestion, Luce."

"Thanks."

"So, any news from Sam?"

"Uhh, you were there for the train wreck at the gym two days ago, right?"

"Yeah."

"Well, the facts are all there. He doesn't want to forgive me or have anything to do with me. So, I'm just going to have to let it go. I mean, I wish I knew what I was thinking in August. Maybe all that heat got to my brain."

Molly shrugged, "At least you have the Line."

Lucy smiled wistfully, "And that will have to do."

Fifth period that week was weird. The percussionists were practicing in the gym and everyone was trying to do their part to act as part of a whole. The effort came out in a bizarro way. The drummers were being exceedingly and uncharacteristically polite to each other. In a section known for its constant insults and play fighting, it seemed the guys were trying to out "nice" each other. Whether phony or not, the results were worth it. After a last run through of the show, each section was honestly congratulating another on its outstanding performance.

By band practice on Thursday, the word had gotten out about the non-school sanctioned "field trip" the drummers were taking. The word had also gotten out about the competition the past weekend and its disappointing conclusion. Lucy was glad to hear a lot more of the band members coming out to support the Line this weekend. She hoped they were able to make their fellow classmates proud.

The percussionists had decided to go to the concert right after practice on Thursday. They were going to caravan so that the younger drummers could ride with the upperclassmen. Through a little bit of persuasion and a few white lies ("Mom, I have to go to the concert or I'll get kicked off the Line!"), the entire Forrest Hills Drum Line was going to the Green Day concert.

Lucy had two freshmen (Morty and Thomas) and a sophomore (Kevin) in her car, all of who were on the cymbal line. Somehow, they had all become fast friends on the field this season. Before marching out for the opening set of the halftime show, they had developed a weird ritual, which mostly involved singing (and what was becoming a choreographed dance) to the lyrics of "Back that Ass Up" by Juvenile. No one knew exactly how it had started, but Lucy and her boys had been bonded ever since.

Finally, they arrived at the concert. After climbing what seemed like a million stairs, the percussionists found their section. The opening act was finishing. After ten minutes while the stage was reset and Green Day started their show. Hearing their Indoor show played by the actual band was awesome! Even the most socially backwards drummers were up and jumping around before the show was over. When the concert finally came to an end, the Line walked out as a group and instantly began reliving the concert on the walk to their cars—talking about their favorite songs and how good this would make them sound on Saturday. The ride home seemed to go by in no time. Lucy had the album blasting and she and the guys were singing along at the top of their lungs with the lyrics. Lucy dropped off the younger drummers at their homes. As she drove home, her eyes glanced at the phone, willing it to ring, but her mobile remained silent.

The away game Friday night went well—the football team beat a really difficult opponent and would be advancing to the State semi-finals. Also, after the success of the Green Day concert, the Line was recharged and ready for Saturday's competition. The ride back from the game was cold and quiet. Back at the school, the drummers didn't have to move their equipment back into the band room, with the competition the next day, they would just leave their drums on the truck. The competition tomorrow was further away than last weekend's, so they would be getting an early start—the report time tomorrow was 8:00AM. After last week's weather, the drummers were taking lots of precautions. They had been watching the Weather Channel all week, and according to the local meteorologists, it looked like clear, but cool temperatures for the weekend.

Lucy had a difficult time going to sleep that night. With all of the craziness and drama of the past weeks, it was difficult to imagine that tomorrow was the last time the Line would be in competition mode for the season. This time tomorrow night, they would just be back to marching the half time show and doing parades. Lucy knew the reality of that wouldn't hit her until sometime next week … probably not until the football team lost and they would put their equipment away for the last time. But tomorrow? Lucy had pride in her previous Indoor competitions but somehow it was different this year—running the drill and moving on the court. She could only hope their hard work would pay off.

25

DON'T LOOK BACK IN ANGER

The Guard/Color Guard n. A group of people used as additional visual effect to the band's performance, adding to the total package that is a March Band. Using flags, ribbons, rifles, and dance steps, the Guard is to the eyes what the band's music is to the ears. Auditions are usually required to be a part of this section.

Lucy was so paranoid that she was going to miss her alarm, that she set two extra clocks to wake herself the next morning. It didn't matter—she was so excited that she literally woke up every hour on the hour through the night and was wide-awake before her alarm went off at 7:00 AM. Lucy quickly jumped in the shower, finished her morning routine in record time and was on her way to the school.

The bus ride to the competition was one of the most memorable Lucy had ever had. Someone had thought to bring speakers for their iPod and the entire bus jammed to the *American Idiot* album during the trip—singing and playing along with the tracks. In what seemed no time at all, the Line had arrived at the competition. Like previous Saturday, the individual competitors went to get their equipment out and start warming up. It was a perfect November day. Cool, clear and crisp. Not a cloud in the sky.

Like the week before, Lucy followed Tom to help with his quints. After Lucy had helped Tom onstage, she went backstage to wait for him to finish and help get his equipment back on the truck. Lucy looked around and noticed Sam, who was warming up on a Real Feel pad under a tree in the distance. Her heart skipped a beat when she saw him.

He's not yours any more …

Lucy had done enough crying in the past week that she had no more tears to shed over the South Washington Captain. She turned around to check on Tom and walked right into Nevada. Instead of moving aside, Nevada held her tight.

Lucy looked up at him curiously, "And just what are you doing?"

"This—"

Lucy saw Nevada's lips coming towards hers and freaked out. She pushed at his shoulder. Nevada did not seem to take the hint. Lucy had to literally avert her face from his.

"Seriously, Nevada, let me go."

"Lucy, quit playing hard to get! I've put up with your attitude the past two weeks and it's getting annoying."

"I am not playing hard to get! I am not playing anything."

"Is something the matter here?" a voice asked from behind them.

Lucy saw Nevada's eyes hazel look up and narrow. He answered, "No, it's personal, we don't need your help."

"I'm not sure Lucy agrees with you."

"I don't—"

Nevada interrupted, "Lucy doesn't know what she wants."

Lucy continued to struggle and said desperately, "I do so!"

Something happened behind Lucy and she quickly found herself spun around and slamming into Sam's broad chest. She looked up, cocked her head and said, "Thanks."

"No problem," Sam moved her behind him and Lucy peeped out over his shoulder. This close to her ex-boyfriend, she inhaled his scent, trying to memorize its subtle parts—his musky aftershave, the just washed scent of his white t-shirt …

Nevada pushed up his sleeves, "Lucy belongs with her own drum line."

Sam answered calmly, "I think Lucy belongs wherever she wants to be."

A third voice joined them, "Back off, Petersen."

Nevada spun around to see Jerm behind him, arms crossed.

"What gives, Jerm?"

"I think you've done enough. I'm not getting our Line kicked out this close to legitimately kicking Sam's ass."

Nevada glared at Jerm, but backed down and walked off.

Sam held out his hand, "Thanks, Jerm."

His former enemy shook it, "No worries. Just see to it that my star second bass player gets to her warm ups on time, ok?"

Sam nodded and they both watched Jerm walk away. Sam cleared his throat, "Hey Luce?"

"Yeah?" Lucy tried to keep the hopeful tone out of her voice.

"I think I owe you an explanation."

"Why is that?"

"It's just, well, I've been burned in the past and seeing the two of you together, I just wasn't sure I'd be able to take it again."

Lucy said as neutrally as possible, "I'm not going to cheat on you, Sam."

Sam raked a hand through his hair, "So, I don't know, maybe we could just start all over?"

Lucy didn't think she had heard him correctly, "What's that?"

Sam gently put his arms on Lucy's shoulders and forced her to look into those intensely dark blue eyes of his, "Because here's the thing. The past two weeks have royally sucked. Leaving you on the dance floor wasn't the smartest thing I've ever done. I've thought about it and I don't want anyone to come between us. Lucy, I want you to be my girlfriend."

Lucy's heart started beating faster. She had waited so long to hear someone say those exact words to her ...

Not just any someone ...

She looked up into Sam's eyes and smiled at his familiar face. She traced a finger over his chin. He understood her in a way that a lot of people wouldn't. She grinned, "I'd like that."

Sam kissed her gently on the lips. When Lucy opened her eyes, Sam was smiling down at her.

After changing in the deserted women's locker room and catching Molly up with the day's events, the girls walked out to meet the guys and start to prepare. The warm up went well and everyone was primed for Preliminaries. Stepping on the court, Lucy got the rush she always felt ... her heart started pounding and each sound was intensified. Everything else in her life drifted away and she had a sense of clarity before the show started. She couldn't wait until tonight when the gym was full and it was really on. The show began. It seemed like just a few moments had passed when they were right in the middle of the mallet toss. *Success!* None of the basses had dropped. Hearing a round of applause from the audience, Lucy knew their hard work had paid off. She heard various applause for the other section breaks.

As great as they did, it was still difficult to wait out the judges' decision. Finally, the announcer began with the individual results from the morning. Lucy wasn't sure who to cheer for, so she just decided to put all of her energy into screaming for Tom. It was a Forrest Hills sweep—Jerm, Tom, Nevada and the cymbals had won.

When it came to the competing Lines, all the usual players had made it to Finals. South had edged out Forrest Hills for first place, but they hadn't won by a large margin. The Lines drew to see when they would compete. South would go last, and Forrest Hills would go second to last. In a matter of hours, the first place Drum Line trophy would be awarded.

26

SHE'S GOING THE DISTANCE

In-step n. *To achieve a uniform look and perfect drill scores, during a performance competitive marching band members must all be on the same "step." When a Drum Major starts a show by marking time, the band should all begin with the same foot thus when they begin marching, each members foot would hit the ground at the same time. If a member does not accomplish this, they are said to be "out of step."*

For the last time that mattered in the season, the Line warmed up. Henry didn't say anything. He didn't need to. The Line was more than ready to go in and kick some ass. They had all the motivation they needed. They wanted to hear their Line's name being called when it was time to announce first place. The seniors wanted to leave their legacy. The juniors, many on their instruments for the first time in competition, wanted to prove themselves. The sophomores didn't want to let anyone down. The freshman had dreams of starting a four year winning streak.

All was quiet as the Forrest Hills Drum Line stepped out on the court. In the brief moments before the show began, Lucy looked out into the crowd and smiled warmly at the band members that had made the trek to support the Line. Lucy's green eyes swept over the audience and saw parents and friends. She got a wink from Henry, who had taken a seat in the front row. This was it. It seemed melodramatic, but the season really did come down to these few minutes. All the practicing, all the bitching, all the hours spent on a court, going over drill and music came down to these precious minutes. Lucy looked to the seniors and for once, did not envy them. While it was fun to be the reigning class, it also meant graduation. Lucy was thankful that she had another year ... another show to learn ... another Line to compete with. Time went by too fast sometimes. It seemed like just yesterday she was standing in the band room, auditioning. Now, she was a seasoned member of The Battery. No matter what happened, Lucy was suddenly very proud of herself. She was here. She had held up her fifth of the bass line.

"Is the Forrest Hills Drum Line ready to take the court for competition?"

Jerm waited a dramatic few seconds before stepping out and gave the cue for everyone. They were ready.

"You may now take the court for competition."

The show started. Like a dream, from "American Girl" to "Boulevard of Broken Dreams" to "Novocain" and ending on "American Idiot". Lucy heard bursts of applause for the section breaks. As much as she wanted to grin, the code of the Line was, of course, no smiling—just concentrated "We're-going-to-kick-your-ass" looks. And then it was over, and they were scrambling to get off the court so they wouldn't get any violations on timing. They passed South's drummers in the narrow hallway that led to the court. Nothing was said between the lines. Forrest Hills was ecstatic at their performance, but weren't about to let South know that, and South was in their pre-show concentration mode.

As soon as Forrest Hills' drummers were outside backstage they started whooping it up. Everyone was congratulating everyone else.

What a difference a week makes …

It didn't matter what the judges said, at least for the next few minutes, these drummers felt like they were the best Drum Line in the world.

With the exception of Jerm and Tom, the Line loaded their instruments into the truck in record time. As was the custom of most competitions, the winning percussionists on each instrument would be giving an encore performance of their winning solo. With only a half hour between the last performance and the awards, Forrest Hills went into the gym to wait and cheer on their fellow drummers.

"Please welcome first place individual tenor winner, Tom Finnegan, to the floor." Tom was wearing a traditional Tom outfit. Dark jeans, white shirt, two tone Doc Martens and his favorite flame suspenders. Lucy smiled, noting that Tom had even added his blue and white striped conductor cap for the evening's event.

Tom started and did not disappoint. To the usual routine he added juggling and for this night's performance, Tom somehow managed to incorporate taking a picture of the crowd on a disposable camera without missing a beat. The crowd was eating it up. Lucy was glad to see Tom getting what he loved—audience recognition. Tom finished to a thundering round of applause.

"Finally on the court this evening, please welcome our first place snare drummer, Jeremiah Stanford."

Jerm began to play his entrancing and technically difficult solo. He was also greeted by a thunderous round of applause. While Jerm cleared his snare off the floor, the Captains and Lieutenants from each of the competing Lines walked down on the gym floor. Representing Forrest Hills High School were Jerm, Doug, Nevada, Lance, and Molly.

The announcer said, "As always, we'd like to thank the Lines for coming to compete today and all the friends and family that support them. A special thanks to the Drum Line Instructors, for all their hard work and dedication to the Lines present today. And now, the results."

Lucy was sitting next to Tom, who had just returned to his seat. They both weren't sure which way things were going to go this evening.

"In third place overall with a score of 98.75, Swiss County High School."

The Swiss County Captain stepped out to accept his trophy with a big smile on his face, he knew next year there would be a lot of returning members from his line and they would be a force to be taken seriously.

"In second place overall, with a score of 99.00 ... South Washington High School."

Sam stepped out, a half grin on his face. He knew that his Line would blame the judges and the "jerks" from his girlfriend's school, but deep down he knew that Forrest Hills had done a better job this evening and in the long run, he felt like he was really the winner. He had Lucy and being with her was better than a plastic trophy any day. Furthermore, his Line had just as many wins as Forrest Hills' and he had an individual snare win to his credit. There was no shame in any of it. He shook hands with the judges.

"Finally, in first place, with a score of 99.5, Forrest Hills High School!"

Tom and Lucy jumped up and hugged each other—they had won! The Forrest Hills section was going crazy. Jerm walked over and accepted the large trophy for first place.

The announcer continued, "Now, we would like to announce the best section captions. In these categories, there are only first place trophies. For these sections, the judges all noted outstanding playing from all the percussionists. These awards are given for musicality, incorporating visuals, and the cohesiveness of the section. The members of the sections should be very proud of this honor. First we would like to award the trophy for outstanding Front Line, the award goes to ... South's front ensemble."

Lucy's heart went out to Molly, but if Lucy knew anything, she knew that it would only give her that much more determination for the next year to totally kick some Pit ass! It was the difficulty of being Pit section leader. You were forever "graduating" your best players to The Battery and always having to teach the next generation of drummers how to be normal members of the Line.

"For cymbals, the award goes to Forrest Hills's cymbal line!"

Almost before the award was given out, Forrest Hills's name was on everyone's lips. Consistently Forrest Hills was pushing the envelope for cymbal visuals and technique. It seemed no one could touch them. Nevada went out to accept the award and held it aloft for all his cymbal players to see. Lucy held her breath, Basses were next.

"For best bass line, the award goes to Forrest Hills High School!"

Lucy, Nathan, Mark, and Jared went crazy. All the sectionals and practice had paid off! Lucy couldn't wait to put her "Best Bass Line" patch on her drum line jacket. She was practically glowing she was so happy. Lance walked over to accept the trophy and looked up to salute his section.

"Next we have tenors, tonight, the trophy goes to Swiss County!"

Lucy wasn't surprised. It was acknowledged that the Swiss tenor line was very seasoned and made up of all seniors. The quints didn't take it too badly. Everyone knew they would be back next year with a strong showing.

"Finally, we have the snares, the award goes to …" The judge fumbled with the paper, "Well it looks like we have a first here. There is a tie. Would the representatives from the Forrest Hills and South Washington snare lines please come up to accept their awards?"

Sam and Jerm eyed each other, but walked forward to accept the trophies.

"That concludes the Indoor competition for this year. Thank you to all our competitors on a wonderful job and congratulations to Forrest Hills for their first place win."

Just like that, it was over. The Line swarmed the court. Lucy and the rest of the basses gathered around Lance, looking at their trophy.

Lucy announced, "Group hug!"

The basses all smiled and joined in. After breaking the hug and walking around the floor in a daze, Lucy felt a tap on her shoulder, and glanced up to see Sam.

"What's up?" she asked shyly.

"Jerm and I decided to officially bury the hatchet tonight. Our Lines are all going to meet up at WaHo."

"Sam, that's great!"

He nodded, "I'll see you there."

The drummers took over the local Waffle House that night. After placing her order, Lucy began to get nervous when she realized that both Nevada and Sam were missing from the restaurant. She leaned over and asked Molly, "Have you seen Nevada?"

"Sorry, I haven't."

Lucy nervously chewed her fingers and kept her eyes locked on the front door. She looked away for two seconds and was laughing at one of Tom's jokes, when she glanced at the door and took a sharp breath.

Molly, sitting next to her, followed Lucy's eyes to the door. With identical bloody noses and smiles on their faces, Nevada and Sam walked in together. The rest of the drummers were so involved in their conversation and celebration that they didn't even notice. Sam slid in next to Lucy at her booth.

Lucy asked, "What happened?"

Sam picked a french fry off a nearby plate, "We settled our differences."

Molly winked, "At least you didn't use wasabi."

Lucy was still dumbfounded, "Are you okay?"

Sam gently blotted his nose, "Nothing a little ice won't fix."

Lucy shook her head, "You would think that after three years of being around you guys, I would learn a thing or two about you, but no, I can honestly say I have no clue how your brains work."

"Just kiss it and make it better," Sam grinned.

Lucy shrugged and leaned over to kiss her boyfriend.

During Homeroom on Monday, Lucy was only just coming down from the high that the weekend had produced. It was sad that the season was over, but looking back, it had definitely been an interesting one. She was suddenly aware that her teacher was calling her name, "Lucy Karate? I have your Homecoming pictures, dear."

Lucy tore open the envelope and grinned at her and Nevada's happy smiles, committing the images to memory and then tucking the pictures deep into her messenger bag. They were memories of an unforgettable season. Lucy pulled out her calendar ...

How many days until the next season starts?

Fin.

978-0-595-42281-4
0-595-42281-0